Dice

The Perished Riders MC - Book 5

Nicola Jane

Copyright © 2022 by Nicola Jane

Cover © using stock images from Shutterstock 2022

All rights reserved.

No portion of this book may be reproduced in any form without written permission from the publisher or author, except as permitted by U.K. copyright law.

Meet the Team

Cover Designer: Charlie Childs @ Cosmic Letterz Designs
Editor: Rebecca Vazquez @ Dark Syde Books
Proofreader: Jackie Ziegler
Formatting: Nicola Miller

Spelling Note:
Please note, this author resides in the United Kingdom and is using British English. Therefore, some words may be viewed as incorrect or spelled incorrectly, however, they are not.

Disclaimer:
This book is a work of fiction. The names, characters, places and incidents are all products of the author's imagination. They are not to be construed as real and any similarities are entirely coincidental.

Dice can be read as a standalone, but it is the fifth book in The Perished Riders MC and therefore would make more sense if read as part of that series.

A note from the Author

This book contains many triggers, including violence, cults, and kidnapping (not by the MC). My bikers are sometimes outspoken and often curse, and I have no control over them. It's also worth noting that this is in no way related to real life, and although lots of research went into cults, the information in this story is not based on any particular cult, and it in no way represents any of my own beliefs.

Contents

Playlist:	IX
CHAPTER ONE	1
CHAPTER TWO	14
CHAPTER THREE	29
CHAPTER FOUR	41
CHAPTER FIVE	55
CHAPTER SIX	67
CHAPTER SEVEN	80
CHAPTER EIGHT	98
CHAPTER NINE	112
CHAPTER TEN	126
CHAPTER ELEVEN	139
CHAPTER TWELVE	156
CHAPTER THIRTEEN	172
CHAPTER FOURTEEN	186
CHAPTER FIFTEEN	197

CHAPTER SIXTEEN	207
CHAPTER SEVENTEEN	220
CHAPTER EIGHTEEN	232
CHAPTER NINETEEN	245
Arthur - A mafia spin off from The Perished Riders MC	251
1. A note from me to you	258
2. Books from this Author	260

Playlist:

Hold My Hand – Lady Gaga
   Happy Ending – Demi Lovato
   It'll Be Okay – Shawn Mendes
   Commander in Chief – Demi Lovato
   Radar – Britney Spears
   Bad Things – Cults
   Wicked Game – Chris Isaak
   I Didn't Know – Sofia Carson
   When I Look at You – Miley Cyrus
   Holy – Justin Bieber ft. Chance The Rapper
   Sorry Not Sorry – Demi Lovato
   Need You Now – Lady A
   I Was Made for Loving You – Tori Kelly ft. Ed Sheeran
   Somewhere Only We Know – Keane
   Slow Hands – Niall Horan
   We Belong Together – Mariah Carey
   You & I (Nobody in the World) – John Legend
   You Mean the World to Me – Freya Ridings

Brave – Ella Henderson

CHAPTER ONE

DICE

I clench my jaw, close my eyes, and take a slow, calming breath as I keep the dice tight in my grip. "Give me a number between one and six," I say, without opening my eyes.

"Please," whimpers the pathetic shitbag.

"One and six," I yell, opening my eyes and fixing him with a hard stare.

He sniffles. "Two," he mutters.

I give him a satisfied smile. "Two, good number." I loosen my grip on the pair of gold cubes in my palm and give them a light shake. Bringing my fist to my mouth, I blow for luck, something I've always done. I throw the dice, watching as they go up in the air, spinning slowly as they fall to the ground and clatter, rolling across the dirty concrete and crashing against the wall before landing neatly side by side. I take a step closer, peering at the black spots, and I wince. "Unlucky."

"No," he growls. "Please, I can sort this out. I know I can, but if you kill me, I can't."

I laugh. "Kill you? Who said anything about killing?" He glances nervously at the table where my bag is, my gun sitting neatly on top.

"Is it in my hand? You don't need to worry until it's in my hand. Now, let's talk."

"It's not as easy as you think to just bust her out of that place. It raises questions, and even if I did it, she'd never speak to you."

"She needs persuading."

"She's straitlaced, the kind of girl who's waiting for the right man."

I grit my teeth. "I *am* the right man—she just doesn't know it yet. The fact she's a good girl is the reason I need her." He frowns and it pisses me off. I'm sick of being looked at like that . . . like I'm fucking crazy. "I rolled a three. Wanna know what that means?" He shakes his head, and I grin. "It means I get to remove at least a third of your pinky."

"Come on, man," he cries, struggling against the restraints that hold him to the chair. "Please."

"I researched it, and you don't even need that finger. It does nothing." I shrug. "Unless you rest your mobile on it when you're flicking through social media." I stare at him for a second. "You don't look like you use social media, but I'll let you choose the finger. I'm easy." I go over to my bag and take out a knife. He struggles harder, this time making panicked pleas.

The door opens and Rosey bounces down the steps, humming one of her annoying tunes. She smiles sweetly, coming to a stop right beside my guy. "What'yah doin'?"

"None of your business. Get the fuck out."

"Maverick sent me to find you."

"And you just happened to know I'd be here?" I ask, arching a brow in her direction.

"I followed you. I was curious."

"You're obsessed," I mutter, taking the guy's hand to keep it steady, even though it's tied down at the wrist. He panics and begins yelling. Rosey rolls her eyes and slaps a hand over his mouth.

"I'm not obsessed. Maybe I'm bored?" She thinks about it and then nods. "Yeah, I think that's it. My mum used to say I was nosier when I got bored."

"Your mum was a whore. Did she even notice you?"

"Ouch, rude!" She watches as I bring the knife to his finger.

"You should tie it off," she says, and I pause.

"Huh?"

"You've got a white shirt on. You wanna tie the finger off, so the blood loss is less."

"No, I don't," I snap. "I know what I'm doing." I line the knife up just below the knuckle of his finger.

"Clearly, you have no idea. And why the little finger? What's the point?"

"Mind your business!" I growl.

"If it was me, I'd take the thumb."

I release the man's hand and sigh heavily. I can't concentrate with her going on in my ear. "Sorry?"

"The thumb," she repeats. "Think about it, there's so much you can't do without your thumb."

I notice the guy's gone quiet. He's passed out from the stress of the situation. I know how he feels—Rosey can cause a lot of stress. "Like?" I humour her.

"Wank," she states, nodding eagerly, and I almost laugh. Rosey slaps the guy, and he wakes with a start. "Hey," she says, smiling wide, "which hand do you use to masturbate?"

"I don't have time for this. Go away," I snap.

"What did you do to piss him off anyway?" she asks him.

"He wants me to persuade my friend to go out with him."

I groan, and Rosey laughs hard. "Are you shitting me?" she asks. "You wanna take a man's finger because you like his friend? Fuck, if she finds out, do you think she'll want anything to do with you?"

"She won't find out."

"He's gonna tell her," says Rosey.

"I won't," the guy promises.

"See, he won't," I say with a satisfied smile.

"Of course, he will. How long have you been friends?" Rosey directs her question his way.

"Forever," he admits.

"Forever! He's gonna tell her."

"Then I'll take more than his finger!"

"Take his thumb and his finger . . . definite wank stopper," she says, nodding.

"How about this," says the guy, and I'm thankful for the distraction from Rosey. "I'll bring her to your bar. Dice's, right?" he asks, and I nod. "I'll bring her tonight. You can charm her."

"She doesn't go to bars," I point out.

"What kind of woman doesn't go to bars?" asks Rosey, looking shocked.

"The good kind," I mutter.

"What do you want with a good girl?" she enquires, smirking.

Rosey wouldn't understand my need for pure and clean, my fascination with normal, everyday women who stick by rules and laws and have never seen bad things. "Okay, bring her tonight at eight. But I swear, if it doesn't work—"

"I'll slice off my own damn finger," he hisses as I cut the ropes from his wrists.

Once he's free, I hold out a hand for him to shake. He frowns, taking it cautiously. "No hard feelings, Cameron, you just got caught in the crossfire."

Rosey follows me back from the warehouse I own, a street away from the MC. All the brothers bought up the land surrounding the club, mainly cos we don't want neighbours rocking up and disturbing our life. And also because we always need buildings for storage or hiding things.

"I can help you with this woman," she says.

I laugh. "No chance. Stay away from her."

"Oooh, I'm intrigued. Who is the person getting you all hot under the collar?"

"None of your business. I mean it, Rosey. She's not from this world, so leave her alone."

"Then why d'yah want to get involved?" I ignore her, and she skips past me. "Fine, I'll show up and ask her myself."

I grab her arm and pull her back to me. She slams against my chest, and when she rears back, she's got her gun pointed to my head. "Try it, I dare you." She grins.

I smile. She'll never shoot me and get away with it. "I'm asking you nicely, Rosey. Stay away from Astraea."

"Astraea," she repeats. "Nice name." She tucks the gun away as I release her. "I'm serious, maybe I can put in a good word."

"No."

"You're no fun."

I'm agitated and I can't help it. She's late. We agreed on eight and it's almost twenty-past. "Everything okay, boss?" asks my bar manager, Stacy. I nod, not daring to speak because I know I'll snap. Finally, I spot Cameron entering the building. He looks nervous as fuck, and the second his eyes meet mine, he pales. Astraea isn't behind him. She's nowhere to be seen, and my fists curl into tight, angry balls. I keep my eyes fixed on him until he's standing before me.

"Let me explain."

"Where is she?" I ask through gritted teeth.

"Outside."

A sense of relief washes over me as I release the breath I'd been holding. "Okay. Well, bring her in."

"The thing is, she's not feeling well."

"Is she okay? Is she hurt?"

"No, nothing like that. I gave her a drink to help her relax, but it might have been too strong. She's never really had alcohol so—"

I don't wait for him to finish before I'm pushing people out of the way to get to her. Cameron is behind me, still trying to explain. When I set eyes on Astraea, hunched over by the wall with her head in her hands, I almost combust in an angry panic.

"Why did you give her alcohol?" I growl, keeping my distance from her and holding Cameron back.

"She didn't want to leave with me, she was uptight and stressed. What was I meant to do? You made it clear what you'd do if I didn't get her here, so I did what I could."

"By getting her drunk without her knowledge?" I hiss. "Get over there and see if she's okay!" I shove him forward, and he stumbles over to Astraea while I linger behind.

"Hey, chica, how are you feeling?" he asks, gently placing his hand on her upper back. I itch to remove it.

"Oh, Cam, what did you give me in that drink?" she murmurs, not bothering to raise her head.

"It was a glass of Coke, Astraea. I'm not sure what's happening."

"I told you it tasted funny," she whispers. "I think it was off."

"Let's go inside and get you some water," suggests Cameron.

She shakes her head and immediately regrets it, groaning aloud. My cock twitches. "I can't go into a bar," she whispers.

"Of course, you can. The Lord won't strike you down for having a glass of water in a bar."

"No, but if my father found out, he'd—"

"He won't. Come on, Astraea, live a little."

"You can use my office," I say in a gruff voice. She looks up, letting her eyes trail the length of my body, and when they reach my face, her head is tipped so far back that she falls onto her arse with a humph.

She grabs Cameron by the arm and pulls him close. "Cam, there's a giant behind you," she whispers, flicking her eyes at me every so often.

"He's my friend," Cameron lies. "He owns this place. I told him you weren't feeling well."

"Where did you find a giant to befriend?" she asks, furrowing her brow. Man, she's cute.

Cameron laughs, hooking his arm under hers and tugging her to stand. She's wobbly, grabbing the wall for support. "I don't feel so good," she murmurs.

"Can you walk?" I ask. She shrugs, and I waste no time scooping her into my arms to carry her to my office. She giggles and the sound washes over me, making my heart beat double-time. Finally touching her after months of watching, longing to have this moment, makes me wanna never let her go. And it feels just as amazing as I knew it would.

ASTRAEA

I don't remember the last time I felt so bad. The room is spinning, and I feel sick. The kind of sickness you get when you've spun around in circles for too long or travelled over bumpy roads for miles. The giant marches through the bar with me in his arms like a ragdoll as people automatically move when they see him coming. He kicks open a door and we're in an office space. When the door closes, the noise from the club drowns away but leaves my ears ringing. At home, I'm not allowed to play music. My father hates it and much prefers silence.

The giant lays me on a worn-looking couch and steps back, staring down at me with interest. I've seen that look before in men's eyes, but it's wasted on me. I'm saving myself for my husband-to-be. Cameron comes into view, standing beside the giant. "Do you think she'll be okay?" he asks him.

"No thanks to you." The giant's voice is deep and growly, and I smile to myself. I like it.

"I overdid it," says Cameron, wincing.

"Yah think?" The giant produces a bottle of water and crouches beside me. "Here, Astraea, drink this. It'll help."

I take it with a shaky hand and half sit, all the time he remains beside me, close enough that I can smell his musky aftershave with a hint of cedarwood. I shake my head, clearing thoughts that have no place creeping in. It's not like I haven't met a handsome man before, but it's usually the kind introduced by my father.

I take a few sips and spill some down my chin. The giant moves swiftly, and I flinch. He frowns, slowing his hand as it approaches my face, and gently swipes away the water. The touch is so careful and soft, it feels barely there, but it's enough to send a thrill through my body, causing me to inhale in surprise. "I have to go," I whisper.

"Soon. You'll be in trouble if you go home like this," he replies, smiling. I can't help but return it. He's even more handsome when he isn't scowling.

"Maybe you should go and grab yourself a drink," says the giant, giving Cameron an annoyed scowl.

"He can't leave me," I protest.

He holds up a set of dice. "Pick a number," he whispers. "If I can roll it, he goes."

"Six," I reply, and his breath hitches. "It's my lucky number."

"Six it is," he murmurs, blowing on his hand before rolling them out onto my stomach. "Well, would you look at that. Cameron, ask for Stacy and tell her I sent you. Order whatever you like on the tab." He says it all with his eyes fixed on mine, and for some reason, I can't look away, even as Cameron leaves me alone with this stranger. The door opens and music fills the room as Cameron slips out, and once it's quiet again, the giant trails his fingers over my stomach and collects his dice. "How did you do that?" I ask.

"I didn't. The gods chose, Astraea," he says, adding a smirk.

"You know what my name means." I say it as a statement.

"The purest goddess. The virgin goddess of innocence, purity, and precision."

How does he know that? It's the first question most people ask when they meet me, because it's so unusual. "You know your history?"

"I was forced to go to god school as a kid. Bunch of nutjobs, if you ask me." He stands, turning away.

I push myself to sit farther, placing the bottle of water on the floor. "You don't believe in god?"

"Only my own."

"There's only one god," I say.

"Says who?" he asks, turning back to me. "Your father?"

My smile falters. "Do I know you?"

He takes a breath and releases it. "Is that your first drink?" I frown and glance at the water. "I mean the alcohol," he adds.

"I haven't drunk alcohol."

"Trust me, Six, you have. What you're feeling right now is drunk."

I shake my head, horrified. "No, I had a glass of Coke or two. There was no alcohol. I don't drink."

"Is that your choice or aren't you allowed?"

"I should leave." I stand, wobbling when the room spins. The giant's there in a flash, grabbing my hands to hold me up. "You look like a god," I whisper.

He smiles. "And you're a goddess, so that means . . ." He trails off, leaving the sentence open.

CHAPTER TWO

DICE

"How was it?" asks Rosey, bouncing towards me as I enter the club later that evening.

I roll my eyes. "Go away."

"I've been waiting for you," she says. "I wanted to see if it went well."

"It went just fine."

She makes a show of looking behind me. "But she isn't with you."

"No."

"Which means she's either very important, or it didn't go well at all."

"What you need is a hobby," I tell her. "Join a book club."

"I have a hobby," she says, smiling wide.

"Stalking me or the other guys doesn't count."

I head up to my room, and to my annoyance, she follows. I try to close my door to block her, but she slips her tiny frame in like she didn't even notice. "Firstly, my hobby is much more exciting than following you, and secondly, I'm not stalking you."

"Hate to break it to you, but you've followed me into my bedroom, can't get more stalkerish than that."

"Did you follow Astraea into her bedroom? Is that why you're home so soon? Did she kick you out in an outrage?"

"If you must know, she ain't that type of woman. She wasn't well tonight, so she went home."

"And you didn't take the opportunity to look after her? Nurse her back to full health?"

"Like I said, she's not that type of woman. Her friend was with her to make sure she got home okay."

"Did he keep all his fingers?"

"This time."

I'm staring up at the ceiling when Pres passes my room and spots me. He slows, sticking his head round the door. "You okay, brother?"

I nod. "Just things playing on my mind," I reply.

"Your mum?" he asks.

"As per usual," I mutter. "You ever think I'm crazy, Pres?"

He smirks. "Aren't we all?"

"I've tried to move on."

"And clearly you can't. Seeing them again after all this time was gonna bring it all to the surface. You gotta do what you gotta do. And we're all right behind you, Dice, you know that."

"Thanks, Pres." I sit up. "I'm gonna head out for night watch."

"You want a brother to ride along?"

I shake my head. "Nah, the place has been quiet for weeks now. I'll call if anything changes."

I roll to a stop just up the road from the place I've been watching for the last month. Part of me wonders if I'm crazy, and the other part hopes I am, so this isn't real. I'd give anything for it to just be a bad memory.

It's ten minutes before the small metal gate opens and closes and Talina makes her way towards me. Her hood is pulled up and her shoulders hunched. She gets to me and stops, keeping her head lowered and her hands stuffed in her pockets. "You okay?" I ask.

"I've got a date," she mutters, shifting uncomfortably from foot to foot.

I pass her the packet of white powder she so desperately needs. She practically snatches it and stuffs her hand back in her pocket. "What about a name?" She shakes her head.

"Three months' time, the ceremony will go ahead."

"Three months," I snap. "So, that's why they're back?"

She nods. "I think so. They don't plan on staying forever. I overheard them saying they can't wait to leave this place."

I nod, feeling anxious. It means I'll have to speed things along, and that means another visit to Cameron. "Thanks. All quiet in there tonight?" I ask, motioning towards the hidden village.

"It's training night, so just the usual, but only three women."

"Not her..."

"No, but you know that's coming too, right?"

"Not if I can help it," I mutter. "You need a ride?"

She looks back at the gate she just exited before nodding. I offer her the spare helmet, and she climbs on, her tiny hands gripping my kutte.

I stop at her house ten minutes later, and she climbs off. Staring at the rundown place she calls home, where she lives with her mum, I ask, "Will you be okay?"

She shrugs. "I guess."

"You need me to come in and check the place is empty?" Her mum has all kinds of men coming and going through the night. In her line of work, it can't be avoided. That's why she needs the powder—keeping her mum topped up gives Talina a quieter night.

"No, it's fine. I'll sort her out and lock myself in my bedroom. Thanks, Dice."

I nod, and she heads inside. I wish she'd let me help her get out of this hellhole, but she won't leave her mum, and her mum won't leave this life. It's too late for her.

I return to my original spot, this time getting off my bike and sneaking in through the same gate Talina exited. It's like a secret entrance. I head straight for the cottage at the side of the church and use the back door to let myself in. The thing about these places is they're too wrapped in their own world to think a stranger would come in.

Cameron isn't too happy to find me waiting for him when he gets home. "How the hell did you get in?" he snaps, rushing over to the blinds and lowering them.

"Careful," I warn, "I can roll the dice a second time and you better pray I don't get two sixes."

He visibly swallows and removes his dog collar. I hate those fucking things, and I stare at it in the bowl beside his keys with disdain. "How can I help you?"

"Is she okay?"

"Yes . . . no . . . I don't know. What exactly do you want with her?"

"You're her only friend, right?" I ask, leading the way into his kitchen.

"She's very sheltered here, but they trust me to watch over her. She's very important to The Circle."

The Circle. Even the name pisses me off. It's a cult, plain and simple. "I have to get her out of there."

He almost laughs until he sees I'm serious. "There is no getting out."

"You're gonna help me."

He backs away, shaking his head. "I can't take them on, and you've lost your mind. I had to fake my own calling to get them off my back. I just want a quiet life."

His reluctance to help reminds me of the fear I once had of The Circle. I shut it down. "You know what will happen to her?"

"She'll get married and live a happy, fruitful life."

"Bullshit, and you know it. How many girls have you befriended just like her? And how many of them went on to lead that life?"

He glances to his front door. "Keep it down," he hisses, knowing someone could be passing right outside and he'll be reported. "Why her?" he snaps. "Why are you so interested in her? If you know all about The Circle, then you know there are more girls just like her."

"I don't need to answer your questions," I growl. "Just bring her to me tomorrow. Same place at noon."

"I can't do that. I can't just click my fingers and take her. They're going to start preparations soon, and then I'll hardly see her at all."

"Which is why I need you to bring her to me!" I yell.

Cameron takes a breath, quickly peeking through a slight gap in his blinds. When he's happy it's all clear, he turns back to me. "Look, I don't know what you want with Rae. I don't know why you're so invested in The Circle. But I do know that no good will come of it. They're not the sort of people you mess around with. Trust me, my father is one of them."

I smirk. "Yeah, well, my mother was once just like Astraea, and if it wasn't for them, she'd still be here today. Noon tomorrow, Cameron, or things might get ugly for you."

ASTRAEA

"Sit up straight, girl!" Father's booming voice makes my head hurt more, and I wince, straightening my spine to its full length. "Cameron needs your help again today. He's having a bible reading around noon."

"Actually, Father, I don't feel too well."

"Nonsense. I've already told him you'll be there, and we don't let our family down."

"Of course," I mutter, feeling my shoulders drop with disappointment. I feel terrible, my head is pounding, and whatever was in that drink last night is responsible. The sting of my father's slap makes it ten times worse, but I don't scream. That'll only earn me another. Instead, I apologise and sit taller.

My brother, Ares, joins us late, which would be unacceptable if it was me, but because he's male, the same rules don't apply. His wife walks two steps behind him with her head bowed. When he pulls out her seat at the table and she lowers, I notice a slight wince in her expression, like she's in pain. "Good morning," Father greets. "Did you sleep well?" He sniggers and a knowing look passes between the two.

"Very well," Ares replies. "And Primrose was grateful for the floor. Thank you, Father."

"Thank you, sir," she murmurs, glancing up slightly to reveal two black eyes. It doesn't surprise me. I'm used to seeing her in this state, mainly because she defies Ares all the time. I'll never defy my husband like that because I know what can happen.

After breakfast, we go to morning prayers. In The Circle, we have our own prayer books. They're deeper than the Bible. At least, that's what we've been taught. I've never read the Christian Bible to compare.

I spend the rest of my morning collecting vegetables for dinner. We grow everything from seed in our back garden, and it's my responsibility to look after them. It's the only pleasure I have here, and I take great pride in it.

Just before noon, I change and head over to Cameron's to help with his bible group. There are a lot of members in The Circle, and he holds many groups throughout the week. But when I arrive, there's no one there, just Cam looking anxious. He smiles with relief when he sees me. "I didn't think you'd come."

He takes me by the arm and leads me to the back room, where the door leads out to his waiting car. We often go through here when we want to explore outside the grounds. It's something we've done since Cam learned to drive. My father doesn't know, no one does, and Cam assures me they'll never find out. If they did, we'd both be in big trouble. I'm not allowed out beyond my home or the church. If I want to go other places, which I never do, I have to take a chaperone, usually a related male.

"Where are we going?"

"We should thank my friend," he tells me, bundling me into his car. "For helping us last night."

"He said I was drunk, Cam. What was in my drink?"

"I have no idea," he says, shrugging. "Maybe they were spiked?"

"By whom? Weren't the bottles sealed when you brought them?"

"You must have had an out-of-date drink." He drives the rest of the way in silence, and I can't help but wonder why he's being so weird with me.

We stop outside the bar. I remember being here last night and crouching right by the wall. "Exactly how do you know this man?" I ask, staring at the brightly lit sign announcing the name as Dice's.

"He was asking me about The Circle. I think he'd like to join us."

"Really?" I gasp. I've never known anyone to join The Circle from outside. Most members are older with kids who were born into it.

I follow Cam inside. It's not open to the public because there's hardly anyone around but bar staff stocking the place. "Can I help you?" asks a female, smiling. I admire her makeup and tight outfit. I've never worn anything so revealing. It's not allowed.

"I'm looking for Dice," says Cam, and I frown. What kind of name is that? Then, I remember the giant holding a set of dice, and suddenly, the bar's name makes sense.

"It's Cameron, right?" she asks, and he nods. "Go right through, he's expecting you."

The giant is behind his desk. He's much more handsome than I remember, with tattoos crawling up his skin. I could imagine the punishment if Father caught me here talking to this man. He screams sin, and there's a definite sparkle in his eye that belongs to the devil.

"Six," he says, leaning back in his chair and appraising me with his eyes.

"We came to thank you for last night," says Cam. "For helping us."

"How's your head?" he asks me, ignoring Cam.

"Sore," I mutter, feeling my cheeks turn red.

"I forgot something in the car. I'll be right back," says Cam, smiling at me before heading for the door.

"Erm, Cam?" I whisper-hiss, glaring at him. He knows I can't be alone with this stranger. My memory from last night comes back again, and I frown. He left me last night too.

"Relax, take a seat," says the giant. "Dice, by the way."

I cautiously lower into the chair opposite him. "That's a strange name."

He grins. "Says the woman named after the pure goddess."

"You're named after number generators," I say, arching a brow, and this time, he laughs. It makes me smile in return because his laugh lights up his whole face and makes him look a damn sight less angry.

"I want to learn more about your beliefs," he explains.

"Cameron can help with that."

"I don't want Cameron to help me. I want you to."

I shake my head. "I can't do that. You'll learn pretty quickly that women can't do that sort of thing."

"Why?"

I hesitate. Outsiders don't understand the way we do things. Father says it's why we can't go out, because we'll be heckled or led astray. "Men are the leaders. They teach, and we learn."

"Wouldn't you like to teach?" I shake my head. The very thought is preposterous. "Shame, I think you'd make a good teacher."

I glance back at the door and lower my voice before admitting, "I used to want to be a teacher when I was small."

"Wow, what a coincidence. Well, I think you'd be great at it."

Cameron is taking too long, and Dice must sense my unease because he stands. "We can go and find him if it makes you feel better." I nod, also standing. "Or, you could spend a little time telling me more about The Circle. He won't mind."

"It really isn't my place."

"You believe in god, though, right?"

I nod. "Yes."

"Like a Christian?"

I shake my head. "Not exactly. The Circle teaches from the real bible. The Christian version isn't the original."

"How do you know?"

I frown. "Because that's what we're taught. The Bible is full of sin. Ours isn't."

"So, you've read the Bible?" he asks, reaching into his top drawer and pulling out a tattered version. He holds it out to me, but I make no move to take it.

"Well, no, I don't need to."

He shrugs and then flicks through the pages. "And in your version, women don't teach?" He smiles, moving closer. He smells good, real good. "Do you go to work, like a job?" I shake my head. "And you wear clothes to cover yourself up," he says, reaching towards me slowly. I watch his large, tattooed hand inch closer to my shoulder, where he runs a finger over the frilled material of my collar. "And you don't wear makeup," he adds, gently stroking the same finger along my jawline and over my cheek. My breath hitches as sparks tingle in the places he's touched.

I've never been touched by a stranger, especially not a male one.

"It hides your beauty," I mumble. Jumbled words from our teachings flit through my mind, and I know I should ask him to remove his hand from touching me, but the words don't leave my lips. Instead, I stare up at him in wonderment.

"I agree with that one," he whispers, cupping my jaw and rubbing his thumb over my cheek. "And you aren't allowed to be alone," he whispers, moving closer still. I stare at his handsome face inches from my own. It's like I've been bewitched and can't look away. "With strange men."

I shake my head, not daring to speak. This is the closest I have ever been to another man, if you don't count the interaction last night, which is blurry in my own mind. "So, you've never been kissed," he murmurs, his eyes flicking to my lips. I shake my head, subconsciously running my tongue over them.

"Boss, can I shoot?" comes a voice from behind me. It's like a bucket of ice has been thrown over me, and I step back quickly, catching my foot in my dress and stumbling back. Dice catches me, wrapping his huge arms around my waist and tugging me hard against him. I feel it, and so does he, and we both lower our eyes to a bulge in his pants. My eyes bug out of my head, and my face burns red with embarrassment.

"Yes," hisses Dice, glancing over my shoulder. "Go."

"I should leave . . ." I whisper, bringing his eyes back to me.

"I wish I could do this without upsetting you or scaring you," he whispers, still gripping me to him. I take a second to process his words. "Unfortunately, it's unavoidable. But know it's for you. It's all for you, Six." He places a cloth over my face, and I try to shake it off, moving my head from side to side, but he pins me against him tighter, turning me away from him so he can hold the cloth there despite my struggles. It smells strong of chemicals, and the last thing I see, as my eyes close, is Cameron watching from the doorway with a brown bottle in his hand and an apologetic expression on his face.

CHAPTER THREE

DICE

I stare down at Astraea in the back seat of the car. She looks peaceful even though her brow is slightly furrowed. "Will she be okay?" asks Cameron from beside me.

I slap him hard on the back, and he winces. "She will now, thanks to you."

"What do I tell her father?"

"Exactly what we practised. Your prayer group got cancelled, so you sent her back home."

"They'll never believe she ran away. She's not the type."

I shrug, carefully closing the car door. "I don't care what they believe."

"I remember you," he mutters, and I make my way to the driver's door, trying to remain calm despite the urge to cut out his tongue. "It took me a while, but I remembered because you were as obsessed with her back then as you are now."

"Goodbye, Cam," I say, getting into the car.

He bends to look through the open passenger window. "You should tell her the truth."

I shake my head and start the engine. "She doesn't remember me."

"Neither did I, you've changed so much. Remind her, Malachi."

The use of my Christian name makes me shudder. "It's too late. She's spent too long under them. I have to take my time and unpick the damage they've done to her."

He nods sadly. "I'll try and call later to see how she is."

I nod. "Thanks. I'm sorry I got so heavy with you. I needed to get to her, and there was no other way."

"Back then, when we were kids, I loved you like a brother. You could have just told me who you were, and I would have helped anyway."

"Brothers would remember each other immediately. Besides, I didn't know if I could trust you."

"I never swayed. Everything we said and what we believed, I never swayed. I still feel the same."

"Yet you're still there, spreading their lies, keeping their women in check."

"I don't know anything else," he mutters, looking guilty.

"Neither did I, yet here I am."

I drive away, leaving Cameron staring after me. He's right, we were like brothers when we were kids, both stuck in the same pits of hell. When you're born into The Circle, they make you believe there's no other way, until you disappoint them, and then they cast you aside.

I drive around the back of the club to avoid any passers-by. Astraea is still out cold, and as I lift her into my arms, my lips graze her head. I breathe in her scent and everything inside me calms. She's like a soothing balm to the chaos in my head. I go inside and walk right into Hadley, who eyes Astraea cautiously. "Club business," I mutter.

"Is she okay?"

I nod. "She'll come around soon enough."

"Righttt . . . well, call if you need me." And she rushes off, not wanting to get caught up.

I'm sitting beside my bed watching her every breath, and when she finally blinks her eyes open, I relax. She doesn't immediately move anything but her eyes, taking in her surroundings. When they land on me, she sucks in a sharp breath and suddenly scuttles back into the corner of the bed, looking terrified. I place my hands out in a placating manner. "It's okay. You're okay."

"Where am I?" she demands.

"You're safe here, I promise."

"I don't even know you," she yells, sounding panicked.

"Where's Cameron?"

"He's gone back."

"I want to go back. Take me back now!"

"You can't go back there, Six. It's not safe."

"I'll scream," she threatens, and I almost smile. "I mean it."

"It won't help," I say, shrugging.

She screams. It's loud enough to wake the dead, but this place is huge, and I can't imagine anyone passing by will hear her. Even if they did, they wouldn't bother. The MC is a noisy place to be.

"All you're gonna do is hurt your throat and probably piss off my President."

She stops and a tear rolls down her cheek. My heart aches. "Please," she whispers. "I won't tell anyone what you did, just let me go."

"You'll understand why. I'll explain it all in time. But I promise, it's for your own good."

"Tell me now," she demands. "Because I can't think of any reason good enough that you'd steal me from my family. My father will be so angry."

"I don't care about your father, Six."

"Stop calling me that," she begs as more tears escape down her pale cheeks. "Why are you calling me that?"

"It's your lucky number, remember?"

"But it isn't my name."

"It's the name I'm giving you, Six, so get used to it. Would you like some food?"

She shakes her head. "I just want to go home."

I stand, and she pushes farther back against the wall like she's terrified. "I have a meeting. Try and rest. I'll be back soon."

She suddenly rushes forward, kneeling on the edge of the bed and almost making a grab for me. "You can't leave me here."

"I can't take you into church, darlin'. No women allowed." This seems to pacify her, and she lowers onto her backside. I guess that rule is something she's used to hearing. "There's someone sitting right outside. If you need anything, knock on the door and they'll get me," I tell her.

"You're locking the door?" she asks sadly.

I nod. I can't risk her running out of here and trying to make her way back to that fucked-up hell.

Church is packed with brothers today. We all wanna end The Circle, and we've been looking at plans for months to try to find a way in. Mav slams the gavel down to get the meeting started and we all fall silent.

"Dice got the girl today," he tells everyone, and relief is evident on their faces. "It was sooner than we planned, but sometimes things happen for a reason. A date had been set for three months, so training would have been starting any day and we would have missed our chance. How is she, brother?" he asks me.

"Scared, confused. The plan was to get to know her and slowly change her mind about The Circle, but as that's no longer an option, it's gonna make my job a lot harder. Trust has already been broken, so I've gotta rebuild that."

Maverick nods in agreement. "Remember what the therapist said about taking things slow. We don't wanna screw her head up any more than what they've already done, and when she's ready, we have help on standby. Sessions might help."

"Do you think they'll file her missing?" asks Ghost.

I shake my head. "I doubt she's even registered anywhere. That's how they get away with not putting their kids in schools or going for health checks. No one knows they exist outside of the cult."

"Is this revenge?" asks Copper. "Cos I know you say you wanna help the women there, but you only took this one, so is this about your mum?"

"Does it matter?" asks Mav.

"I guess not, Pres. It'd just be nice to have full disclosure. This girl is one of their leaders' daughters, right?"

"I can't deny I want to see him suffer," I admit. "Taking his daughter, the purest of his crop, will cripple him, and yeah, I'll take great delight in telling him I have her. But it's about stopping them, making sure they never kill or hurt another woman."

"And you're sure that's what they were gonna do?" asks Tatts. "It all sounds too crazy."

I hate he's questioning me, and my expression shows it. The whole damn reason I never went to the cops was cos I realised how fucked-up and far-fetched it sounds. "Yes. They believe sacrifice brings them power. They make an offering to their god and look for signs of acceptance. It's all crazy. They make it suit themselves. Astraea going missing will be seen as a punishment from their god. At least that's what her father will probably tell them. I ain't certain if he believes it all or he's just made it up to suit his sick desires."

"Fuck, you hear about this shit in films," mutters Copper, "but not in real life."

"My mum lived it, trust me. They used to take girls, vulnerable ones. That's who they'd sacrifice because they knew no one would come looking. After my mum fucked up, they decided in-house breeding for their sacrifices was less hassle. Astraea, and all the girls like her, won't be registered anywhere. They won't have gone to school with The Circle using their own male teachers to home-school the kids. Everything is very controlled."

"And they've kept her this long why?" asks Ghost.

"She's the ultimate sacrifice. They used to teach the boys separately when I was there. They'd tell us about a goddess to cleanse the souls of all the rulers, and so all girls are generally kept until teenage years. Once menstruation begins, that's when they're at their purest. But Astraea was always seen as special, and her father would spout off shit about him producing the ultimate purest offering. She has to stay pure until her twenty-fifth birthday, hence why the date was set for around then."

"You know a lot about it all to say you left when you were a kid," Grim points out.

"They hammer those teachings into you from the minute you can speak," I mutter bitterly. "I witnessed my first sacrifice at age ten. And at age thirteen, they expected me to become involved in the ceremony. Luckily, they discovered I wasn't blood-related to any of them."

ASTRAEA

My heart beats fast and hard in my chest. I can hear the whooshing in my ears. I've checked the door and the windows more than once to see if there's any possible way I can escape, but they're all tightly locked. At one point, the man from outside opened the bedroom door to ask if I was okay, and he looked so terrifying, I gave up, because I didn't want him chasing me down.

I wander around the room. It's clean, which I find odd for a man. Not that I've seen any man's bedroom before. I check my watch. My father will expect me for dinner in one hour, and when I don't show, he'll be angry. Maybe Cam will raise the alarm? Although he didn't seem too concerned right before the psycho giant put me out.

I open a dresser drawer and peer inside. It contains boxer briefs. The next is full of clothes. I sigh heavily. I'm scared of the giant, but I'd rather he was here answering my questions than gone, leaving me to overthink.

In the bathroom, I open the cabinet and pull down a bottle of aftershave, unscrewing the cap and inhaling the citrus, woody scent that's completely owned by him. It warms my insides, and I close my eyes, allowing myself to enjoy it for a second. We don't use perfumes or makeup, and the men don't smell of aftershave back home. The Circle likes everyone to remain fresh, clean, and natural. I remember my mother wearing clear lip gloss one time. I was only small, but my father was so angry, he beat her. I remember his hateful words as his fists hit down on her hard. He was embarrassed his wife would dare sully what our god had given her.

"You thinking of drinking that?" I jump at the sound of the giant's voice, and the bottle slips from my hand, crashing against the tiles and splintering into tiny pieces, spraying the liquid up the walls and across the floor.

"Oh my goodness, I am so sorry," I wail, dropping to my knees and trying to gather the broken glass into a pile. "I am so sorry," I repeat, panic taking over.

"Six, it's fine," he says, crouching down to try and catch my eye.

My father would get so angry at my clumsiness, promising to one day rid me of it. "I'm so accident prone, I shouldn't have been touching your stuff," I admit, wincing as the aftershave gets into the tiny cuts I now have from scooping the glass.

"Please," he says firmly, and his hands take my wrists, "just stop."

I swallow, remaining still as I stare at the mess on the floor. "I'm sorry," I add one last time.

"It was an accident. It's not a problem."

"If you have a dustpan, I'll clean it up."

He shakes his head, smiling kindly. "No. Leave it. I'd like to sort your hands."

My eyes fall to my hands facing palm up and still being held by his large, tattooed ones. Blood pools around each individual cut. "They sting," I whisper.

The giant looks at the shattered pieces of glass on the ground. "I don't want you to injure your feet, so I'm going to lift you onto the counter so we can rinse your hands under the water. Okay?" I nod. His boots crunch on the shards as he steps closer, and then he effortlessly lifts me to sit beside the wash basin. He turns the cold tap on and guides my hands under the running water. After a few minutes, he lifts each hand at a time to examine them. "I don't think you got any glass in there," he says, running a thumb over each palm. He opens the cabinet and reaches for a first aid kit. "Let's go dress these." He once again lifts me, carrying me back into the bedroom.

"I can replace the aftershave," I mutter.

"I don't need you to."

"I have no money on me, but when you take me home—"

"You can't go home, Six."

Dread fills me again. "I don't understand."

"You will. In time."

I watch as he places a soft pad on one palm, securing it with tape. "I can't stay here," I say, attempting to make him see sense. "My parents will be worried."

"I know they will. Your mother especially. Your father might be, but for different reasons."

"Do I know you?" I ask. His words give me the impression he knows a lot about me and my parents.

"You used to."

I frown for a second, trying to remember. There have been so many people who've come and gone from my life, mainly female, and then it hits me. "Malachi," I whisper. It's the only male I have ever known to disappear from my life. I pull my hands from his and scoot back onto the bed, putting distance between us. My father warned me about him, fearing he'd return one day to take me from The Circle. He nods, confirming, and I begin to cry. The tears fall without a sound leaving my body. I cried so many tears for this man, just a boy when I knew him. He left and that was that, and we weren't allowed to speak of him again. But before that, Malachi was my friend, my very best friend, and I missed him. I'd spent years wondering about him and why he left with no explanation. "You left," I whisper accusingly.

"I didn't have a choice, Six."

"Get out," I mutter. "Leave me alone."

"They lied, Six. They told you lies about me."

"Get out!" I scream, and he grits his teeth together, the way he would before, when the men used to hit us or yell. "I need to think," I add, calmer this time. "You've surprised me. I just need a minute." He nods once, his expression sad, and then he leaves, locking the door behind him.

CHAPTER FOUR

DICE

I roll the golden cubes, and when they land on five and two, I snatch them up and shove them inside my pocket. "What does it mean?" asks Rosey, pulling herself up to sit on the pool table.

"Huh?" I didn't even know anyone else was in the room. I've been so lost in thoughts, I've paid no attention. The look on Six's face when she realised who I was, was one of pure terror. I knew The Circle would probably fill her head with bullshit about me. We were too close, and they would have wanted to ruin her perception of me to stop her asking awkward questions.

"When you roll those things, what does it mean? Say they land on matching numbers, does that give you an answer?"

"I'm not in the mood, Rosey," I mutter.

"Why do you do it?"

"I just do."

"If you roll double six, what does it mean?"

"Let's see," I say, bringing them from my pocket again and holding them up. "I roll a double six and I can kill you."

She grins, a sparkle in her eye. "And if you don't?"

I blow on my hand before throwing the cubes onto the pool table. They clatter and bang together before rolling to a stop.

"Then you get to live." I scoop the one and three up. "Lucky you."

"That's kind of hot," she says, biting her lower lip. "How's your prisoner?"

"Taking a moment to remember," I mutter, rolling the dice between my fingers.

"Dice, the prospect said she's asking for you," shouts Copper from across the room.

When I get back to my room, Astraea is sitting by the window. "They made an announcement in church," she says. "They said you'd been brainwashed."

"Not true. They were the ones brainwashing."

"But they were right," she snaps, glaring at me. "Look at you. Look at what you're wearing and the tattoos on your skin. You have aftershave—"

"Had," I cut in, smiling, and she glares harder.

"There are condoms in your drawer," she says accusingly, pointing to my bedside cabinet.

I can't hide my smirk. "How do you know what those are?"

"They were in that magazine you showed me once."

I grin. "We got up to some mischief." I remember finding the magazines in my mum's bag. We'd spent ages scouring them before we burned them. They were on the banned list in The Circle, and I was worried my mum would get caught.

"You corrupted me," she accuses. "I didn't know it until you left, but I realised you'd been brainwashed all along."

"Bullshit. You were just as bad as me at wanting to escape that place. All three of us would look for ways to get out."

"That's why Cameron didn't stop you taking me. He was in on this!"

"Six, you saw it too. You knew The Circle wasn't the truth, and it's not. It's a cult. They teach you their ways and their beliefs to keep you in The Circle, but that's not normal life. There is freedom."

She shakes her head. "I don't want freedom. I have a life back with them, and I like it there."

"You hated it," I remind her. "You'd dreamt of leaving and becoming a teacher."

"Women don't teach. Men teach, and women learn."

I scoff. "What did you learn, Six? Tell me what you've learned."

"That god loves me. That he protects me, and he'll guide me back to my home."

"Or maybe he guided me to find you and rescue you?"

"No, I have a purpose, and it's to be special in The Circle. I have a duty to the Lord—"

"You don't. It's a lie. They're lying to you."

"I don't want to talk about this anymore," she whispers, tears filling her eyes again. "Please take me home."

I shake my head, annoyed she doesn't want to listen. "I never wanted to leave you," I mutter.

"But you did, Malachi, and my life became better. I listened to the teachings, and I know my calling. I have a purpose." She sighs and looks out the window. "When you first went, my father told me you might come back to try and take me away. He kept me inside for a very long time after that. He told me the devil had twisted your mind against The Circle."

"I tried to come back for you, but the place was heavily guarded, and then one day, it was gone. I searched for you, and then a few months ago, by chance, I saw Cameron. He passed me by in the street like a stranger, but I recognised him right away. I followed him, and he led me back to you. I always knew I'd find you, Rae. I never gave up hope."

"We moved around. It became unsafe to stay in one place because outsiders were too curious. At least, that's what my mother said."

My mobile rings and I see Cameron's name. "I have to take this, Six. I'll be right back."

I step outside the room, locking the door. "Cam," I answer.

"I must be quick, her father just left. When she didn't appear for dinner, he was concerned. I said exactly what you told me to, and he's gone to look around the village."

"Okay, good. Play it cool, Cameron. I'll let him know I have her soon."

"Is she okay?"

"She remembers," I mutter.

"That's good, right?"

"Not really. She doesn't trust me. Her father filled her head with bullshit."

"Your mother's story was used for a long time to scare the girls here. Talks of the devil and punishment made sure they didn't speak to outsiders again. Rae sees you as an outsider now, so it'll take time."

"She can hate me forever as long as she's safe."

I stare around the dinner table at Rylee, Hadley, and Meli. "This is so important," I tell them.

Mav nods in agreement. "Tread carefully."

"She doesn't understand and thinks they're very much the only people she can trust. The Circle teaches women that makeup and perfume, books, and modern day technology are all produced to corrupt them."

Meli gives me the same stare I often get whenever I tell anyone about the cult. "It sounds crazy."

"It is," I say. "I've been looking for them for years, and now we finally have them, we can begin to rip it apart. But Astraea can't know any of that. So, if you can avoid talking about The Circle, it would be better."

"What are we gonna talk about if she's not into makeup and books?" asks Hadley. "Do we just talk about the club?"

"We'll figure it out," says Rylee. "Let's just go and meet her. Diamond made cake, so we'll offer that."

"Thanks, babe," says Maverick, and he leans over to kiss her. "I appreciate it."

ASTRAEA

There's a light knock on the door, and then the lock clicks and three women come into the room. One holds out a tray with a cake on it. "Hi, I'm Rylee."

"And I'm Hadley, and this is my twin, Meli," says another.

"We brought cake," adds Rylee, placing it on the bedside table.

Then they stand awkwardly, looking at me. "So," Hadley eventually says, "how are you?"

"Where's the guy, Malachi?" I ask.

"Dice? He's sent us to keep you company."

"Why do you call him that?"

"The guys here all use road names. Dice got his because he uses a set of dice to make decisions," says Meli, and her twin nudges her in the ribs, hard. "Ouch," she hisses.

"Road name?" I repeat.

Meli moves to the window seat, and the other two follow, one sitting on the chair and one on the floor. "They're bikers," says Rylee. "As in, they ride motorbikes."

"It's like a motor vehicle," adds Meli. "It has two wheels and . . ." The other girls stare at her in disbelief, and she trails off. "What?"

"She knows what a motorbike is," snaps Hadley, and I can't help but smile.

"She might not," Meli argues.

"I know," I confirm.

Rylee smiles kindly. "So, these guys are part of a motorcycle club. They all live here and . . . well, drive motorcycles." She laughs, shrugging.

"Where is here?" I ask.

Rylee glances at the other women, unsure how to answer. "London," she eventually says, and relief floods me that I'm at least in the same area as my family. I knew The Circle moved to London just a few months ago. Before that, we were in Scotland. "Have you been in London long?" she asks.

"A few months. My father wanted us back here for my ceremony."

"Sounds good," she replies.

"Do you work?" asks Meli.

"I look after the gardens," I say, thinking about the vegetables I picked earlier for dinner. "And clean."

"You like to garden?" asks Hadley, smiling. "Me too. I'm teaching my daughter, Oakley, how to grow strawberries at the minute. The second they turn red, she picks them. She has no patience."

"We grow all our own fruit and vegetables," I say proudly. "We also have animals, but I'm not so good with those."

"I run a women's centre," says Rylee. "We help vulnerable women."

"Vulnerable women? In what way?"

She folds her legs under her bum on the seat. "Well, I was married to a man who was abusive. He'd hit me and lock me inside our home all day with my daughter. He was very controlling, and I wasn't happy. Since I escaped, I've been helping women just like me."

"How did you escape?"

She smiles. "This club helped me."

"And you wanted them to?"

She nods. "Yes. They're good at helping people."

"I don't need help," I mutter, "if that's what you were trying to say. I'm happy with my parents, and I'd like to go home."

"I'm a lawyer," says Hadley, changing the subject.

"And I help anywhere I'm needed," adds Meli. "At the women's centre, in the bar, with babysitting."

"Maybe you could look after our garden," suggests Hadley.

"I'm not going to be here that long," I say. I know my father will find me eventually and take me home. He needs me.

DICE

"I can't get hold of Cameron," I tell Maverick over the phone. I've been out here for hours and haven't seen a sighting yet. He's not answering my calls or text messages either. "I think we should make our move now, in case he's in trouble."

"Your call. You know these people better than me."

I stare at the entrance to the village for The Circle. There's one way in and one way out, unless you count the back entrance from the church, which is separate, but only Cam and Astraea have been using that. "I think I should go in."

"Not on your own, brother. Wait for me."

I disconnect the call and do as asked. Maverick will be here within ten minutes. I was hoping The

Circle would be distracted looking for Astraea and wouldn't bother Cameron too much, but it's not like him to ignore me completely.

When Mav arrives, I point out the entrances, including the church. "I think we should go into the back entrance to the church and see if Cameron's there first," I suggest.

He nods. "Lead the way."

We walk up the gravel path to the church's back door. It's locked. "There's a broken window," whispers Mav, pointing to a small corner of glass missing from one of the painted windows. He kneels so I can use his leg and pull myself up to look through.

"They're all in there," I whisper-hiss. "All the Lords."

Their long cloaks they wear in meetings and rituals make them look stupid, but when I was a kid, they scared the shit out of me.

I strain to listen. "I think it's safe to say she's been taken. My daughter would never willingly leave. She's very committed to the cause and was looking forward to her training," bellows Astraea's father, Joseph. I recognise his pinched features and his cruel smile.

"And if we can't find her?" asks another.

"It's not an option. She is the most important sacrifice we've ever had. Bring in the girl. We'll ask god for help," he says.

The front door opens and a sleeping girl is carried in. She looks to be in her late teens and doesn't stir when placed on a table before the altar. They form a circle around her, and Astraea's father moves to the girl, gently tugging the white robe she's wearing until it falls open to reveal her naked body. "Where is my vicar?" he yells, and Cameron is pushed towards him. He stumbles, almost falling to his knees, but when he stands, I get a glimpse of his swollen face and blacked eyes.

"They've beaten Cameron," I whisper. "There's a girl on the sacrificial table. She's about nineteen, maybe. Passed out cold and naked. They're going to offer her to their god in the hope he'll lead them to Astraea."

"Fuck's sake. Now what do we do?"

"Cause a scene?" I suggest, jumping down. "I'll get his attention, and he'll send the others away because he won't want them to realise who I am and that I'm back. It'll cause a panic and he'll hate that. You go in and get Cameron and the girl, then I'll meet you at the bikes."

"I feel like we should get back-up."

"The girl will be dead in the next ten minutes if we don't do this now."

Mav grins. "Man, you didn't use your dice."

I hand him my lock pick for the back door. "I had 'em in my hand the whole time," I say. "Now, hit me good in the face. I want them to think I'm a down and out drunk. It'll rattle them."

"Thought you'd never ask," he says, swinging back and punching me without hesitation.

"Motherfucker," I hiss, stumbling back. "You've got way too much pent-up aggression going on."

I pull out my whiskey flask and make a show of stumbling through the main door of the church. "Oh come all ye faithful," I sing at the top of my voice, swinging the flask beside me and crashing into a pew. "Whoops."

"Excuse me, this is a private service," snaps one of the men moving towards me.

"The Lord has enough room for us all," I wail, swishing my flask at him. "This is a church, right?" I ask, looking around. My eyes land on the naked woman and I grin. "Or is it?"

"You need to leave," he says, trying to grab my arm. I swing at him, missing on purpose and falling to the ground.

"That wasn't fair. You moved," I complain. "I need help. I've been beaten and robbed, see?" I point to where my face is throbbing.

"Someone help me get him out of here," the man growls.

"I'm looking for Malachi," I slur.

"What did he just say?" snaps Joseph, rushing forward.

I make eye contact and grin. He narrows his eyes and realisation passes over his face. "Leave," he shouts to the men. "Go and check on our wives and daughters. The devil is in town. Cameron, take her back to her room."

I laugh, but the men don't have to be told twice. They scuttle off like the spineless bastards they are. I spot Maverick and turn my attention back to Joseph. "Shall we step into the office? I don't think your god needs to hear this," I say, leading the way into Cameron's office. Joseph locks the door, and I smile. I'm not the same scared kid I once was.

"Where is she?" he spits.

I laugh. "No warm welcome?" I tuck my flask away.

"I'll slit your throat right now," he yells angrily. His face turns red, and I arch my brow, sighing heavily.

"To think I used to be scared of you," I mutter. "I see you still feed your bullshit to these brainwashed idiots."

"What happens in The Circle has nothing to do with you anymore. You are not a part of it. So, you need to return my daughter and disappear again!"

"That's not gonna happen."

He rubs his brow, a sure sign he's panicking. It's good to see him sweat. "What do you want?"

"To stop you. I've waited so long."

He pulls his knife from the sheath hanging over his shoulder. I stare at the dull blade and wonder how much blood it's spilled since it took my mother's life. "You won't walk out of here," Joseph promises.

"And then how will you find Astraea?" I grin as those words sink in. "If you kill me, she'll die because she's all alone, locked away, and only I know where she is." I head for the door, unlocking it. "I'll be in touch, Joseph. You need some time to reflect, speak to your god, get some advice, but don't spill any more blood, or Astraea will die."

CHAPTER FIVE

ASTRAEA

The shower's been running for a long time and I'm starting to wonder if Dice, which he insists I call him, is still awake. He looked tired when he returned an hour ago. Without a word, he went into the bathroom, and he's been in there since.

I stand, slowly walking over to the bathroom, and roll my eyes. It's silly. Why do I care what he's doing in there, or if he's asleep? My father always said it was my downfall, caring too much. Regardless, I tap on the door lightly. "Are you okay?" There's no reply. I gently push the door with one finger, and to my surprise, it swings back and steam billows out. Then, as it clears, I see Dice sitting on the floor of the shower with his knees pulled up to his body and his head resting on them. The water hits his back, and the skin there is red raw. "Should I get someone?" I ask.

My voice startles him, and he unfolds and stands in one quick movement, looking ready for a fight. My eyes naturally fall to his genital area and widen. I've seen men's parts before—every Sunday, we take turns bathing the Lords in the communal baths—but I've never seen one so . . . big.

Dice grabs a towel and wraps it around his waist. "Sorry, I was lost in thought," he mutters, turning off the spray. "Are you okay?"

My face is burning with embarrassment. "Yes. I . . . erm, I was . . . never mind." I rush back to the safety of the bedroom.

He follows a few minutes later, now dressed in grey tracksuit bottoms but no top. He rubs his wet hair on a towel. "Rylee got you some clothes," he says, pointing to a bag on the ground. "I know you usually wear . . ." He points to my dress. "But she did her best to find clothing to keep you covered."

I pull the bag closer and kneel to go through it. Dice sits on the chair, watching. I pull out a long-sleeved jumper followed by a pair of denim jeans. I've never worn anything like this. At home, we mostly wear dresses that come to our feet. We don't wear undergarments, only when we menstruate, and I hold up a piece of string and frown.

Dice laughs. "It's a thong," he explains. "Like knickers."

"But this would . . . hurt."

He laughs harder, and I find myself smiling too. His laugh is infectious. "Yeah, it doesn't look too comfortable, but I don't think that was why they were designed." Next is a bra and I put it to one side. My breasts aren't big, so I've never needed to wear support. There's a couple dresses, but they're all too short, and there's nothing for bedtime. "I'll see what else she has. Maybe we can go and look at her storeroom. She stocks it for the women she helps, so there should be a better variety there." He gets up and opens his drawers. "In the meantime, you can wear something of mine for bed." He hands me a shirt. "These might be big, but you can fold them at the top," he says, passing me some shorts.

I go into the bathroom and change quickly. I resent that he's brought me here and is keeping me against my will, but a part of me is scared when he leaves. I don't know who else is behind that door apart from the three women who seemed nice enough but didn't offer to help me leave.

I'm relieved when he's still seated in the bedroom. I sit on the bed, and he stares at me with piercing eyes. "Did you like Rylee and the girls?" he asks, and I nod. "They're all really nice here."

"Not nice enough to help me," I point out.

"I can ask them to visit tomorrow," he offers, ignoring my remark.

"Where did you go?" I ask. "After you left The Circle."

"I lived on the streets for a while," he says, "and then I met a woman called Diamond. She helped me and introduced me to her family here. I've stayed with them since."

"In London?"

"Yes. I left for a while when I joined the Army, but London is my home."

"I was sad when you left," I mutter. Cam and I were so confused, but when he didn't return, we believed what they told us, that he'd been brainwashed. It made so much sense as he'd always been the ringleader when it came to disobeying the rules.

"I got you a gift," he tells me, reaching for a parcel and handing it to me. I peer inside a paper bag and pull out a book. "I know you've only read what you were allowed to read, and this is very different from that."

"*The Funny Tales of a Primary School Teacher*," I read the title aloud.

"You said you wanted to become a teacher one day, so when I saw it, I thought of you."

I bite the corner of my mouth to stop the smile I feel coming and slip beneath the sheets. I rest my head against the headboard and open the book.

Light streams into the room, and I open my eyes and immediately cover them with my arm. "Sorry, I brought you some breakfast," says Dice, kicking the door closed behind him as I push myself to sit up. I couldn't put the book down and spent most of the night reading, even after Dice left me to sleep in another room.

He places a tray on the bed, and my stomach growls as the smell of eggs and bacon fill my nostrils. "I like the book," I tell him.

He smiles. "I gathered that, because you didn't put it down from the second you opened it."

"Schools aren't like that in The Circle. Some of those stories are so funny, and a part of me wishes . . ." I trail off.

"I'd like to take you out of the room today," he says.

My heart rate picks up. Leaving the room means I could escape. "Okay."

"Maybe you could meet my President?"

I nod, taking a bite of toast. "He's in charge?" Dice nods. "Did he tell you to take me?"

Dice laughs. "No. Maverick runs the club, but we have our own minds and we can make our own choices."

"Does he mind you keeping hostages here?"

"Hostage?" he repeats, laughing again. "You're not my hostage."

"Prisoner, then," I say.

"I'm helping you, Six. You just don't see it yet."

I shower and dress in the jumper and denim jeans that Rylee got for me. Staring at myself in the mirror, I already don't recognise myself and I've only been here one night. This is what they said would happen if we left The Circle. Outsiders would change us, and we'd become unrecognisable. I shudder, sure that my mother is worried and my father will be so angry.

Dice is waiting for me as I emerge from the bathroom. He's throwing the set of gold dice up and down. "Why do you carry those?" I ask.

"They make me feel better."

"Like a comforter?"

"Sort of. My mum gave them to me. She came home after sneaking out for the evening and had these with her. She'd been drunk, although I didn't know it at the time. She was giggly and . . . happy, I guess." He smiles fondly at the memory. "I have so many memories of her sneaking out and coming home merry. I've spent a long time since, wondering why she didn't just leave and take me with her." He sighs and shrugs, pasting a smile in place of the frown. "Shall we go?" I nod.

He unlocks the door, and we step into the hallway. I suddenly feel nervous, and as if he senses it, he slips his hand over mine and gives it a gentle squeeze. Somehow, this reassures me, and I let him lead me downstairs.

The place is huge. One large room with a bar at one end, there're chairs and tables and large couches dotted around. There're doors leading off, but I focus on the one door I need to make my escape—the exit. It's over by the bar area, which is too far for me to outrun Dice, plus there are people milling around who I'm sure would stop me if he alerted them.

Dice knocks on the door which has the word 'President' on the front. "Come in," yells a male voice, and Dice leads me inside.

A large man sits behind a desk, and Rylee is perched on his knee. She smiles at me, and I return it. "The clothes fit?" she asks.

"Yes. Thank you."

"You look so different," she adds, and it confirms my fear of change.

"We could do with more," says Dice. "I thought I could take her to your storeroom at the shelter?"

She nods in agreement. "It's pretty busy down there today. Could you do it tonight, after closing?" she asks, and Dice nods.

"Pres, this is Astraea," he says, presenting me to his President. "Six, this is Maverick."

I bow my head like I've been taught to do at The Circle. "You don't need to do that here, sweetheart,"

Maverick tells me. His voice is deep, like Dice's, and I raise my head. "We're all equal here."

"But you're in charge?"

He nods. "Only cos these clowns need to be bossed around sometimes. They couldn't function without a leader," he says, laughing.

"So, you can make the decision on if I go home?"

"Six, we talked about this already," says Dice with a heavy sigh.

"But I want to go home, and you won't let me."

"Dice is right, sweetheart. You're better off here, trust me," says Maverick.

"I don't trust any of you," I snap. "I don't know you."

"Have we done anything other than be kind?" asks Rylee gently. "We really are trying to help, Rae."

"Let's go meet some of the others," Dice mutters, leading me from the office.

He takes me to a few other men who all wear the same jacket as him. Back home, our Lords wear robes a lot of the time, or cotton trousers and button-down shirts. A few of the women look me up and down with disdain, making it clear they don't approve of me. Their bodies are barely covered, and their faces are masked behind makeup. I wonder if it's these kinds of women the teachings warned us about, who try and lure men to a darker side.

We're almost by the exit, and my heart thuds in my chest. If I can slip away without him noticing, that would be perfect, but I have a feeling it won't be so easy. Dice turns to speak to a man behind the bar, and I take one step back from him, bringing me closer to my escape. I take another and pretend to look around the room. He doesn't notice. Taking a deep breath, I turn away and make a run for the exit. I slam open the door and run right out, taking no notice of anything or anyone as I focus on the gate that is currently wide open to let in some bikes. I reach the gate and look left, then right, before making the snap decision to run right. My feet burn, as I don't have anything on them but a pair of socks, but I don't notice the stones digging into them because I'm too desperate to get away.

And then I'm lifted into the air and slammed back against a hard body. I cry out in surprise. "Six, what the fuck are you doing?" Dice growls in my ear. His arms remain tight around my waist.

"Please," I beg, "I just wanna go home." Tears of frustration burn my eyes.

"Not gonna happen," he hisses, turning back around and carrying me towards the clubhouse. I fight against him, kicking my legs and twisting to make him drop me, but he holds on firmly. "You keep fighting like that and I'm gonna throw you over my shoulder," he warns.

"Let me go! Let me go!" I scream, and he slams his hand over my mouth. *Why aren't there any people around?*

"If you weren't so fucking pure, I'd put you over my knee and punish you for running like that," he mutters. "I'd love to see your pale arse nice and pink with my handprints all over it." I twist my head, managing to get a chunk of his finger between my teeth, and bite down. He hisses, ripping his hand away and shaking it. "Fuckkk," he growls. "I'm trying to be patient here, Six, but you're testing me." Then, he spins me around and throws me over his shoulder, slapping his hand against my backside. It's sharp and fast, and it takes me by surprise.

"My name isn't Six" is the only thing I can think to say.

"It is now . . . Six."

DICE

I march her back to the bedroom and dump her on her feet. Her cheeks are pink and flustered, and I grin. "Next time I see you with that flushed look on your face, it'll be because I put it there," I tell her. "Now, sit down!" She sits without thinking about it, and that pisses me off further. When she was small, she'd refuse to do as she was told. She'd always end up punished, but she didn't care. "Do you want to sit?" I ask.

"No," she mutters, and then she lowers her eyes to the ground. That pisses me off more.

"Fucking look at me, Six!" I yell, and she does. Again, no questions. Her eyes come straight to mine, but I see it, that defiant little girl trying to get out. "If you don't wanna sit, stand. Tell me to fuck off."

"I want to be alone," she whispers.

"So you can pray? So you can ask your fake god to forgive you because you want to tell me to fuck off, don't you, Six? You want to scream in my face and hit out. You want to defy me." A tear rolls down her cheek. "Say it," I dare her. "Tell me to fuck off."

"No."

"Nothing bad will happen. London won't fall if you curse out loud. God will not strike you down or taint your soul."

"Please go."

I step farther into the room, slamming the door and locking it. "No. I don't want to." I fold my arms over my chest to make my point. "I can't believe you tried to run."

"I want to go home."

"You have no idea about that place. It's not what you think."

"Why do you care? You left, you're free. I want to go home to my family, to my Lords. I want to collect vegetables and cook dinner. I want my normal life back."

"Today was the first day I made a decision without rolling the dice," I tell her. "Letting you out of this room was a big deal, and I made that decision without trusting them."

"Is that what you did the day you took me?"

I nod. "I rolled a perfect double six. A double six means I can save a life or take a life." She lowers her eyes again. "I chose to save one."

"My life was not in danger before you took me."

I snigger. "You have no idea."

"You can't keep me here forever."

"Once you know the truth, you can make your own choices. But until then, you're staying here."

CHAPTER SIX

DICE

I'm angry. I know she's scared, but what the fuck? Running off like that in a place she's not familiar with, it's plain stupid. God only knows what would have happened to her on the streets of London cos there's no way she'd ever find her way back to that shithole.

"What was that all about?" asks Ghost, taking a seat beside me at the bar.

"She's scared. She doesn't know the truth, so I can't blame her."

"You're gonna have to tell her something, brother. It's not good for her to be locked in that room, and once she knows the truth, she can venture out around the club."

I nod. "I will, but I'm too pissed to deal with her now. I guess for me, nothing's changed. She's still the kid I knew back then who wanted to break the rules and run away from that cult. I forget she's been there her whole life, and without me in her ear, she succumbed to them. Her running like that, it felt like betrayal. But to her, it's survival."

"She'll get to the same page as you soon, Dice. You can't just undo all that damage in a few days. The Pres told us they had some girl ready to sacrifice. What exactly do they do?"

"Depends. They make the rules. If they want to fuck, they'll tell themselves they need to cleanse her with their goodness. They'll tell her the gods willed it. Other times, they'll kill them, saying it's an offering to the gods. They believe it cleanses The Circle of evil."

"It's so fucked up. I've heard about cults and shit but never been this close to one. Were they gonna kill Astraea?"

"I think so."

Cameron hardly looks up when I go to check on him. His eyes are swollen to the point of closing and he's exhausted. I remember that feeling well. I spent years being on high alert, and he's been the same. Now he can finally relax, he's fucked. "Just me, brother," I say, taking a seat beside his bed.

"How's Rae?"

"She's fine. She tried to leave earlier."

"You want me to speak to her?"

"Nah, she doesn't know you're here yet."

"How's Ellie?" he asks. The girl they wanted to sacrifice earlier is still resting.

"She's still out for the count. We've got someone sitting by her side twenty-four-seven, so she doesn't panic when she wakes. They drugged her?"

"Yeah. I'm not sure what they use, but the girls mostly come to me like that. She's been training for two months."

"Poor kid."

"Did you speak to Astraea's father?"

"Yeah, just to let him know I'm back. I'll make contact again soon."

"I felt like he already suspected you were. They beat me, saying I let their most precious possession leave. I denied it, of course, but it's like they knew."

"There's no way they could have known. I've been careful."

"Why didn't you just kill him?" he asks, wincing in pain.

"Because it would scare the rest of them. They'd up and leave before I had a chance to get those girls out of there. He wants Astraea, and I want the rest of the girls. We're at a stand-off until one of us makes a move."

"Aren't you worried he'll come for her?"

I grin. "Brother, I hope he does. I'd love for him to try and take her."

Rae is reading when I go to the bedroom. I've decided tonight I'll sleep in the same room. I'm telling myself it's so she can't escape, but the reality is I feel better when I'm near her.

I shower and change without acknowledging her, and when I return to the room, she's put the book down and is sitting cross-legged on the bed. "I want to know the truth," she announces.

"You ain't ready."

"I am. I'm completely ready."

I glare at her. "You tried to run today. That means you're not listening when I say I've done this to keep you safe."

"I might not want to run if you just told me everything. You're a stranger to me and you want me to trust you after everything, including you kidnapping me."

"What did they tell you would happen on your birthday?"

She twists her fingers together nervously. "Erm, that I was having a ceremony. That I would help to cleanse The Circle."

"And what do you think that means?" I sit opposite her on the bed.

She shrugs. "My parents told me I was special, and that one day, the gods would welcome me." She shrugs again. "I don't really know. I trusted them to tell me when it was time, what I needed to do."

"Where is your god?" I ask, and she frowns. "Is he here, on this planet, living amongst us?"

"Well, no, don't be ridiculous. You know, you were there for the teachings when you were younger."

"So, where the hell do you think you're going if the gods would welcome you and you know they're not on this planet?" I snap.

She scowls. "I'm not stupid, Malachi, but it's for the good of The Circle. It's the reason I'm—"

I grab her hands. "It's not," I say, cutting her off. "It's not the reason you're here, or the reason you were born. They tell you that so you go along with their plans." I scrub my hand over my face. "Or maybe they believe it too. I don't fucking know but . . ." I pause. She's staring at me like I've lost my mind, and I sigh. "I believed them too, when I was there."

She snatches her hands back. "No, you didn't. You never believed them. You questioned everything, and you made me and Cam question it too."

"You were the one who questioned everything, Six. You didn't believe them, none of us did."

"I was a kid," she hisses. "I didn't understand. But after you left, I could think straight because you weren't in my ear dripping poison."

I stare for a few seconds. "You think that's what I did?"

"Is it because of your mother?" she asks, her voice low.

I frown. "What do you mean?"

"They told us about her after you left. They said she'd succumbed to life outside of The Circle and you'd gone to find her. Did she do this to you? Did she poison you? If god rejected her because she was no longer pure, it's not The Circle's fault."

I scoff. I knew she'd be hard to crack, but they're so deep in her head, it feels like she's unreachable. "She wasn't rejected, Six, because your god doesn't exist."

She slaps me hard. So hard, it hurts her hand and she yelps, retracting it as soon as it's made contact and holding it to her chest. I suck in a sharp breath and release it slowly. "Go to sleep," I mutter, rising to my feet.

"I'm sorry, I—"

"Now, Astraea," I growl, and she flinches. She slips her legs under the sheets and lowers until her head hits the pillow, all the while keeping her eyes on me.

ASTRAEA

Dice is mad. His cheek is red where I struck him, and as he storms out of the room, my heart twists. I'm like my father and brother, and I'm so disappointed in myself. Rubbing the palm of my hand, it stings. I've never hit out at anyone, not since . . . I smile sadly. Not since Dice was eleven years old and he tried to plant a kiss on my lips.

A few minutes pass, and I'm lost in memories of our childhood when he returns. His cheek is blazing red and I wince. He takes a seat on the bed, and I watch warily as he takes my sore hand and gently turns it palm up, placing an ice pack against it. "I shouldn't have said that," he mutters, keeping his eyes fixed on my hand. "I pushed you too far."

"I spent a long time watching men hit women," I say quietly. "It's not an excuse, but I always wondered what they got out of it."

He smiles, finally looking me in the eye. "Did it feel good?"

I shake my head and a tear slips down my cheek. "It felt horrible. I didn't like it."

He brings his hand to my face and swipes my tears away with his thumb. "I was eleven," he whispers, "and I wanted to make you smile, so I pressed my lips against yours . . ."

"And I slapped you," I finish.

He nods, grinning. "But it worked, because you smiled."

I frown, trying to think back to that day. "Why was I sad?"

He shrugs. "It was so long ago. Back then, you were sad a lot."

"I was?"

He pulls the sheet up higher over my body. "You should sleep."

"My parents will be missing me," I mutter. "They were scared you'd come back for me one day."

"Why do you think that was, Six?"

"They said you'd want revenge."

"My mum was never rejected by god, Six."

"Then tell me what happened."

He shakes his head. "Go to sleep." Grabbing a pillow and sheet from the cupboard in the corner of his room, he throws it down on the floor, then proceeds to make a bed for himself.

"You don't have to stay here. It's not like I can get out," I say, alarmed he'd think about sleeping in the same room as me. "I promise I won't even try."

"Night, Six." He fluffs his pillow and lies down, turning his back to me.

I spend most of the night staring up at the ceiling, wondering what god must think of me. Not because Dice insisted on staying in the room, but because I was secretly happy that he did. I shouldn't want to be anywhere near him, but somehow, I feel safe when he's around. I chant a prayer in my head, the one I was often forced to chant when I was a kid because I was forever doing something my father didn't approve of.

It's almost three in the morning when Dice sighs. "I can hear you thinking," he grumbles from the floor.

I laugh. "I can't sleep."

He pushes to sit. "Warm milk?" he asks. I nod, and he gets up from the floor and holds his hand out to me. I stare at it for a few moments before taking it and allowing him to lead me from the room. As we enter the kitchen, he drops my hand. "There's no point in trying to run, the gates are locked," he mutters, going to the fridge and retrieving the milk. I take a seat, so happy to be out of that bedroom, it didn't enter my head to run this time. I watch as he heats the milk, stirring in cinnamon. "You loved this when you were a kid," he says.

"Please tell me about your mum, Dice."

He pours the hot milk into a mug and brings it over to where I'm sitting. "She was murdered," he says, handing it to me and taking a seat. For a second, I think I misheard. The Circle told us she was cast out because she was no longer pure and god had sent her away.

"When . . . how?"

"She kept secrets from The Circle. They were discovered and the Lords weren't happy," he says bitterly.

"What secrets?"

He hesitates, then continues. "I wasn't born into The Circle like they thought. My father was from outside."

"I'm confused."

"The Circle used to find vulnerable girls, the sort nobody would miss if they were taken." He pauses, letting the information sink in. "My mum was raised in care. She didn't know her parents and had no relatives. She met a man who she trusted, but she was only fifteen and he was a lot older. He took her in, showed her a life where she'd be taken care of . . . in The Circle. Once she was in, they wouldn't let her leave, so she accepted her fate. But she would occasionally sneak off. Just like you." He smiles.

"Anyway, she met another man and got pregnant with me, but he wasn't ready to have a family, so Mum lied and pretended to carry a child from god." I gasp. I knew he didn't have a father like I did. Some of the women in The Circle carried children who were considered to be children of god. All those women lived together in the big houses and raised their children together. The girls would go on to do what their mothers did, and the boys would learn from the Lords. "They only discovered the truth because my real dad came looking for us. He'd decided he wanted to be a father after all. Mum sent him packing, but the damage was done. She confessed her sins, and she paid a heavy price."

I shake my head, unable to believe what he's telling me. "They didn't hurt her. We knew she'd been influenced by evil. They told us she had. They told all the girls in our teachings that we mustn't be alone with men outside of The Circle because that's how evil creeps in."

Dice scoffs. "No, Six, *we're* not the evil ones. *They* are. They murdered my mother."

"To cleanse her of her sins," I say, desperate for him to understand. "So god would forgive her."

"No. Because they were angry she'd betrayed them. She'd fooled them for years, and they couldn't forgive that. She was raped by every single one of the Lords."

"No, you're wrong."

"I'm speaking the truth. You told me you were ready," he snaps. "Why do you find it so easy to believe them but not me?"

I stand. "Because I don't know you."

He stands too, making his way around the table until he's in front of me. He takes my hands and stares deep into my eyes. "You do know me, Six. Better than anyone. You're the only one who ever knew me. You remember," he says, cupping my cheek in his large hand.

"But you left and things changed."

He rests his forehead against mine. "I left because I saw them for what they were, and I won't rest until you see them too, Six."

I'm so confused, and with him so close, stroking his thumb over my cheek and smelling his scent, I can't think straight. My heart is pumping so hard, I feel like he can hear it. His eyes are burning deep into my own, and there's a feeling building inside me that I can't explain. And then his thumb stops moving and his expression changes too. It's one I don't recognise, conflict maybe. Suddenly, his lips gently brush mine, and I suck in a surprised breath, holding it. His other hand cups the back of my head as he touches my lips again, this time slightly harder, and then he tips his head to one side and does it again.

"Jeez, get a room," says a female voice from behind us, and I jump back, putting distance between us. Dice looks over my head in irritation at whoever is there.

"What do you want, Rosey?" he snaps.

"I wondered when I'd set eyes on this beauty," she says, and then she comes into my eyeline. She grins while looking me up and down like I'm on display. I shift uncomfortably, moving closer to Dice. She seems hyper, bouncing on her heels, and that's when I spot blood splatters on her shoes. I grab Dice's arm.

"Fuck, Rosey, you're scaring her. Calm down."

"Sorry, it's adrenaline," she says, shrugging. "I'm Rosey." She holds her hand out proudly for me to shake, but it's also got blood on it, so I make no move to touch her. She looks at the blood, then moves her hand closer to her face to examine it, frowning. "Christ, it gets everywhere."

Dice places his hands on my shoulders and begins to guide me from the kitchen. "Goodnight, Rosey," he mutters warily.

"Oh, come on, she's gotta get used to it if she's staying," Rosey shouts after us.

"Sorry about her," says Dice, steering me to the stairs.

CHAPTER SEVEN

DICE

Since our early morning encounter with Rosey, Astraea has hardly spoken. I watch her from my seat by the window as she reads the book I gave her. "I have to go do some work," I say. I've not been to the nightclub since Astraea came here and the other brothers have had to step up and take over, but sitting here all day while she reads is pointless. She doesn't reply, so I grab my kutte and slip it on. "I have a surprise for you later," I add.

"No, thank you," she mutters.

"You don't even know what it is," I say, laughing.

"You kissed me," she suddenly snaps, glaring at me.

I grin. "Is that why you're hardly speaking?"

"You shouldn't have done that."

I move closer, leaning down until our faces are inches apart. Her gaze flicks back and forth between my lips and my eyes. She wants me to kiss her again, there's heat in those baby blues, and I smile wider. "Didn't you like it?" I whisper, running my tongue over my lower lip. She follows the movement and her lips slightly part.

"No," she murmurs.

"I don't believe you, Six. I think you liked it very much. In fact, I think you want me to do it again." She's breathing hard and her cheeks are flushed. "Imagine how it would feel to have my lips everywhere," I whisper, pressing my forehead against hers. She closes her eyes. "Tasting every inch of you." I pull back, and her eyes shoot open. "See you later, Six."

I groan when I arrive at my club and spot Rosey at the bar. "We're closed," I snap.

She hops off the barstool and bounces towards me. "I know. Stacy asked me to come along and try her new cocktails."

"At eleven in the morning?" I ask, arching my brow.

Stacy comes from the back room and smiles when she sees me. "Hey, boss. How are you?"

"I didn't know we were adding cocktails to the menu," I snap, but I instantly regret it when she gives me a wounded puppy look. She's a great bar manager, and I shouldn't take my mood out on her. "Sorry," I mutter. "What cocktails were you thinking?"

Her smile comes back as she hands me a leaflet advertising two new cocktails. "We have the Rosey," she says, placing a red cocktail on the bar.

"You named a cocktail after her?" I ask, rolling my eyes.

"Don't pretend you hate the idea," says Rosey, taking the cocktail and having a sip. "Oh my god, that's perfect. Smooth, fruity, and cool, just like me."

Stacy smiles, sliding the cocktail to me to try. "It's a coincidence. I picked the name because of the colour," she says. I take it and hum my approval. "Next up is Six."

I almost choke, placing the Rosey back on the bar as Stacy produces her next creation. "Six?" I repeat.

"Your lucky number, right?" she asks, and I nod. "There are six ingredients that make this little beauty," she adds as I take it from her and try it.

I smile. "It's good, Stace. Real good."

She grins under my appraisal. "So, I can add them to the menu?"

I nod and head off to my office with Rosey hot on my heels. "Things looked cosy with you guys last night," she says, and I detect the smirk in her voice.

"Until you interrupted," I mutter, sitting at my desk and opening my laptop.

"You think a girl like her would fuck you on the kitchen table?" she asks, laughing. "Thought you said she was a good girl."

"What do you want, Rosey?" I ask, exasperated.

"Your help."

"With?"

"I like someone," she blurts out, and I groan. "Oh, come on, you're a man, you know what men want."

"I do," I say, nodding, "and it's definitely not a woman who kills men for a living. Talk to the ol' ladies about it."

"No," she huffs. "They give me girly shit to do and it's not me."

"Then speak to Mav. He's the Pres, and weren't you two close?"

"It's weird. I can't go to him. We're mates, you can help me."

I lean back in my chair. "Okay, who is it?"

"Arthur," she says, and I laugh hard. "What?"

"Arthur fucking Taylor?"

"Yeah, so?"

"I take back what I said. He probably would love a woman who kills for a living. I've never even seen you guys talk."

"I think I annoy him," she admits

"That does surprise me," I reply sarcastically, and she narrows her eyes. "He usually goes for," I pause, unsure how to word it without offending her, "glamourous women."

She flops down in the chair opposite me. "I know, that's the problem."

"Just ask him if he's interested, Rosey. He's a straight down the line kind of guy."

"What's happening with you and Goody Two-shoes?"

"Don't call her that," I mutter. "She's got a lot to process." My mobile rings and I'm relieved to get out of this conversation. "Pres?"

"We got a woman here looking for you. She's called Talina."

"She's my inside eyes," I say. "I'm on my way."

Talina looks relieved to see me when I step into the club. "There's another sacrifice tonight," she blurts out.

I steer her in the direction of Mav's office, and we take a seat. "Pres, this is Talina. She's my inside eyes at The Circle."

"How?" he asks, frowning.

"She's not actually part of it. She's a . . ." I glance at her for help.

"Hooker. I'm a hooker," she finishes. "One of the top guys there sneaks me in a few times a week to take care of him and his friends."

"And how do you get information?" asks Mav.

"They think I'm mute," she admits. "It's how I get some of the top-paying customers. If they think I can't speak, they're more careless around me."

"What's happening tonight?" I ask.

"They're offering sacrifices to god for seven nights straight, believing it will bring Astraea back to them."

"But they know I have her."

"Maybe they're trying to bring you out in the open," suggests Mav. "It could be a trap."

"Nah, they're not that clever. Astraea's dad is one of the top Lords. He wants to motivate the other men while he comes up with a plan to get her back. If he manages to get her back in seven days, the disciples will believe in him more."

"Should we go in tonight and save this woman?" Mav asks.

I nod. "How can we not, now that we know?"

"I'll call church. Bring Talina, we might need her help."

The brothers sit in their usual spaces around the table, occasionally eyeing Talina with suspicion. Women aren't usually allowed in church, especially not a stranger.

Mav bangs the gavel to signal the meeting is in progress. "Meet Talina, Dice's inside at The Circle.

She's discovered there will be a sacrifice every night for the next seven nights."

"Which means?" asks Copper.

Mav looks to me for an explanation. "They'll have told the disciples that the offerings are for their god, and if he accepts them, they'll get Astraea back in return."

"And what happens when god doesn't give them back their prized possession?" asks Tatts.

"The Lords will say god didn't accept the offerings and they'll come up with something else. But I think they're planning on getting her back before then."

"Planning will get them nowhere," snaps Grim. "She's safe here."

"What exactly happens at these sacrifices, apart from the obvious?" asks Ghost.

I lean forward slightly. "They'll start with washing her in holy water. The priest will chant prayers while this happens. Usually, she'll be passed out, and when she comes around, they'll rape her. Then, the highest-ranking members, they'll slit her throat and let her bleed out."

"Fuck," hisses Grim.

"And they only get worse as the week goes on. By the seventh day, she'll probably be younger and the torture will be more violent. They keep the girls awake, and when they fight or scream, they spout bullshit about the devil being inside her, trying to take her from them. They'll use all their men to rape her, telling them that they're cleansing her soul for god. It's some twisted shit."

"How old will this woman be tonight? And do we plan on turning up each night, cos they'll be waiting come tomorrow," says Grim.

Talina steps forward. "The seven girls are chosen. That's how I knew. They're being kept in a cell under the church."

"And how did you know about this cell?" asks Cooper suspiciously.

"Brother, she's good," I tell him. "I trust her."

Talina smiles sadly. "I get hired to service some of the men there. It's a secret, so we meet under the church."

"Why the fuck would you do that when you know what they're doing?" Grim questions.

"She don't have a choice," I snap defensively. "Lay the fuck off."

Grim stands, squaring his shoulders. "You forget who the fuck I am?" he roars.

I take a calming breath and shake my head. "Sorry, VP," I mutter. "Talina's mum is an addict, so she does what she has to, to keep their heads above water."

Grim sits back down. "See, that's all the explanation I needed."

"Talina, we can help you and your mum," says Mav, "but we'll talk about that away from this lot."

ASTRAEA

I am so bored. Sitting in this room is driving me insane, and I finished my book hours ago, so when I hear the lock and Dice comes in, I'm relieved, even though I'm still angry with him. However, I'm not expecting Cameron to appear behind him, and I stare, shocked. He's bruised and battered, and my first thought is Dice hurt him. "Surprise," says Dice.

"You beat him up?" I snap, rising to my feet.

"Not me, Six. Thanks for thinking the worst, though."

Cam steps closer. My heart aches because I trusted him, and the second Dice came back, he went against me, tricking me. "Are you okay?" I ask, folding my arms over my chest to stop myself from touching him. He nods. "Who did that?"

"Your father wasn't very happy with me."

I narrow my eyes. He could be lying to help Dice convince me The Circle is bad. "My father would never lay a finger on a priest. You're his connection to god."

"He'd have to believe in god first," Dice mutters.

"Wow, so now you're telling me he doesn't?"

"No, Six. He likes the power, the virgins, and the murder."

Cam glares at him. "Stop," he hisses.

"Well, it's fucking true. I'm sick of her looking at me like I'm the bad one."

"Give us ten minutes," says Cam, and Dice nods, leaving us alone. I sit back down on the bed, and Cam points to the spot next to me. "May I?" I nod, and he lowers to the bed. "It must be really confusing," he begins, "but are you really so shocked, Rae?"

"That you betrayed me and my family?" I snap. "Yes."

"We had talks, didn't we? We questioned if what was happening around us was right. If god really willed the death of those girls."

I pick some imaginary fluff from the sheets. "It was a sacrifice."

"They still died, Rae. I found out they had plans for you," he looks into my eyes, "and I couldn't let them take you."

"I don't want to talk about it," I mutter. "Let's talk about what you did."

"You always do this," he snaps. "You refuse to listen to anything you know deep down is true. We knew it then, when Malachi was in our life before, and we know it now, but we're both too damn terrified to say it aloud. They had it all planned, Rae. You were the ultimate sacrifice."

"Isn't it an honour?" I ask feebly. I knew what my father meant when he told me I was special. The way the Lords watched me when I was sent to bathe them, the heat in their eyes and between their legs. I'm not stupid, but it's my destiny. My life beyond this world would be perfect and I'd be with god.

"I've been there when these sacrifices take place, and there's nothing honourable about them. Dice is right. Those men like power, and if they shade it with stories of sacrifice, they can do vicious things and still hold their heads high. You were bid on," he says, and my mouth falls open. "A twenty-five-year-old virgin, never kissed, never touched. Someone paid a lot of money for you."

"I don't understand," I whisper.

"Your sacrifice wasn't going to take place at the church. You were about to be sent to train with one of the Lords, to ensure you were compliant and so terrified, you'd accept the things that would happen from the man who won you."

"Things?" I repeat.

Cam pulls out a mobile phone. Only the men were allowed to own them in The Circle. He pulls up a video and holds it out. "I recorded this as evidence. I wanted to take it to the police, but Dice has other plans."

I watch a girl I don't recognise being led into our church. She's stood before the altar, where I assume Cam is standing with a hidden camera. I don't know which Lord holds up her arms because his face is covered and his hood is up. Another steps forward and pulls her white dress from her, leaving her naked. She whimpers in protest, and the man touches a stick to her stomach. It emits a small blue spark and she cries out, almost dropping to her knees. Tears wet my cheeks, but I'm too shocked to remove my focus from the video to wipe them. Another Lord takes the girl and lays her on a white stone before the cross where Jesus hangs. She's crying so hard, but she doesn't struggle as he parts her legs and touches her there.

Sickness swells in my stomach as the door opens, I'm startled and almost drop the phone. Dice glares between us, and then his eyes fall onto the device in my hand. "What are you doing?" he asks.

"She needed to see," explains Cam.

Dice's eyes widen and he snatches the phone, staring down at the screen. "You showed her this bullshit?"

"She wouldn't believe it otherwise, Malachi," Cam yells back.

"I told you, my name is fucking Dice," he growls, grabbing the collar of Cam's shirt and shoving him back onto the bed.

I don't think about anything other than the open door, and I see my chance. They're so busy yelling, they don't notice as I slip away and rush down the stairs and straight through the club. A few of the women glance up as I pass, but their reactions to alert anyone are too slow, and I'm out the front door in a second. The gate sits open, and I thank god. *God*, I snort to myself. I don't even know what I should believe. I stop, overwhelmed by the sudden chance to run mixed with the realisation that I have nowhere to go. And then I cry. The tears are fat, and my entire body shakes. Bending slightly, I place my hands on my knees, trying to catch a breath between sobs.

DICE

"Stay here," I warn Cam, who followed me downstairs the second we realised Six had made a run for it.

"Mav's already gone after her," says Rylee.

I step out and spot Mav at the gate. Six is almost on her knees, crying uncontrollably. I make my way over, and when Mav sees me, he shakes his head, warning me to stay back. "It's a huge shock. Your whole life's been a lie," he's saying calmly, "but I have people who can help."

"Did she die?" Six asks, looking directly at me. "The girl in the video . . . did she die?" I nod, and she sobs harder. My heart is breaking for her and all I wanna do is wrap her in my arms, but there's something in her stance that tells me she hasn't decided if she should continue running.

"You could go back there and be like her. They had big plans for you, and it could be way worse than what you just saw," I say. "Or you could stay and let us help you."

"They won't ever give up," she yells. "I was important, he told me all the time."

"Your father?" asks Mav, and she nods. "He can't get to you here," he assures her.

"Did they . . . did they have sex with her?" she asks me, and I nod again. "Why?"

"Because they're evil," I say honestly. "They say they're chosen by god to cleanse the women with their seed." She slams a hand over her mouth and sobs harder. "But in truth, they choose who enters their circle. It's why Cam lied and said he'd been chosen to spread god's words. Being a priest was better than being involved in that. As soon as the boys turn thirteen, they take part. The ones who enjoy it, they get to stay as disciples, but the ones who don't, they're killed."

"But Cam was involved. He was there and didn't stop them. Why didn't he stop them?" she wails.

"How?" I ask. "He was just as scared. He wanted to survive, Six. He lied to survive, so he could be with you, because he didn't want to leave you."

"I think I'm going to throw up," she whispers, looking at me with such sadness, I can't stop myself rushing over to her. I scoop her against me, burying my nose in her hair. She clings to me, sobbing harder, and although my heart breaks for her, I like the way she feels in my arms and how she needs me right now. She feels like home.

It took some time to settle Six down, and in the end, I agreed to let Doc medicate her so she'd sleep and I could get out for a few hours. She has so many questions, and I don't have all the answers. There's only one man who does, and I never want him near her again.

I focus on the village gates surrounding where The Circle is staying. It's privately owned by some rich bastard, and the gates are manned twenty-four-seven, but the men aren't the sort to tackle a rush of bikers. However, tonight, we're going in through the church. Cam gave us keys that open the cellar door as well as the cages holding the girls. "You ready?" asks Mav, walking over to my bike. I nod, taking off my helmet. I open my palm and check the two golden dice, seeing both on six, and I smile to myself. *That's what I thought.*

We slip through the back door, and Mav leads a few of the brothers down to the cellar to help any other girls who might be down there. I lead Grim and Ghost to the front, and peering around the thick red curtain, I see a girl, half asleep, laid on the front pew with men in cloaks standing around. "She's one of our younger girls, pure and tight," says one, and the others snigger.

"Do you think this will please god?" asks another.

"Will Astraea return?" another enquires.

A man marches down the aisle, and the others stand straighter. It must be Astraea's father, but he's got his hood up, making it hard for me to see his face. "Robert flies in at the end of the week. She'll be returned by then, it's god's will."

He grabs the girl's wrist and hauls her up, but she's so drugged up, she can't balance and falls to the ground. He pokes her with the cattle prod, and she screams in surprise. "Get up," he snarls in her face, "or I will make you drink my seed until you're sick."

I can't listen to any more, so I step from the curtain and take a slow walk towards the altar with my arms held out in a similar pose to Jesus. "What do you think? Could I be mistaken for him?"

They all turn to me. "You're back," says Joseph, dropping the girl's wrist.

"I'm a sucker for blood."

He grins. "Virgin?" he asks, kicking the girl's thigh. "I have several waiting."

"Actually, no, you don't, but we'll get to that part."

"Have you come to your senses? Astraea must be missing us."

I grin. "Not now she knows the truth."

"Poisoning her won't make a difference. It won't stop her destiny."

"To be fucked by a bunch of perverts and killed?" asks Grim.

"If you don't return her, you'll all be at risk," Joseph continues as if Grim hasn't spoken. "It has to happen. The deal's been done."

I walk over to the girl, and Joseph steps back, putting distance between us. I grin, knowing he's scared of what I might do should I get hold of him. I pick her up. "Maybe I'll take you to see her before I slit your throat," I tell him, passing the girl to Grim. "I haven't decided yet."

"You can take my seven girls," he tells me, laughing. "I'll just pick seven more."

I blow my hand and roll the dice onto the red carpet. Everyone's attention is on them as they land at the feet of a cloaked man. "What are the numbers?" I ask, and he frowns, peering down closer at the dice.

"Two and five," he mutters, looking utterly confused.

I grin, pulling out my gun and using it as a pointer to count along the line of men. "One, two." Stopping on number two, I pull the trigger. He drops to the ground with a thud, and I continue. "Three, four, five." Pulling the trigger a second time, the fifth man drops next to the second. "Now, I don't wanna cause a scene, but you have to stop with these rituals cos

I'll just keep coming back and I'll just keep killing until there's no more of you left."

I turn and head back through the curtain. "You know, you could just kill him and put an end to it all," Grim points out.

"I didn't roll sixes. It wasn't his time," I tell him, shrugging, and he groans.

"I know Mav said we do this your way, but I don't think he thought it through," he complains. "And what am I supposed to do with her?" he asks, looking at the limp girl in his arms.

CHAPTER EIGHT

DICE

Rylee was amazing. She found places in a shelter for five of the women, and the other two were brought back to the club until she can secure somewhere for them too. I head up to see Six with a bounce in my step, feeling like I've done some good.

The bedroom door is open like I left it, and Six is sitting in the middle of the bed, staring into space. "Hey," I whisper, and she jumps with fright. "Sorry, I didn't mean to scare you."

"Where were you?" she asks.

"I had some business to sort. I've arranged for you to see someone, a therapist. She'll help you understand all this."

"What's so special about a virgin?" she asks, and I almost choke.

"Huh?"

"I want to know what the fascination is."

I smirk. "Six, another time. It's been a long day."

"Longer for me. I've been here thinking over my entire life and wondering what to believe. Everything feels like a lie."

I place my kutte on the chair and take a seat beside her on the bed. "I left the door open so you could leave the room."

She leans back against the headboard next to me. "I don't know anyone."

We fall silent for a few minutes before I finally answer her question. "Virgins are pure, right? I guess that's the attraction. Men are animalistic, wanting what no one else has had, and taking a woman's virginity is special. At least, it should be. And then there's a darker side, men who crave it. Men who take it without consent because the thought of a helpless, shy virgin turns them on. It feels good for them to have all the power."

She stares at her fingers as they knot together while she thinks over my words. "I'm not completely stupid to how the world works," she eventually says, "but I felt safe at home not questioning things. I didn't want to be beaten for seeming like I was questioning our beliefs. If I kept my head down and got on with my duties, things were peaceful. I liked gardening and looking after the home with my mother. And I got used to not being allowed to question my father or brother. But I know about sex and where babies come from. I know they kept some women like my mother to have children for the Lords. I thought one day, I'd marry a Lord also and have his children and my life would just be peaceful."

"It's not how it should be, Six. The things that happen in The Circle aren't normal. And say you did marry a Lord and have his children, what do you think would happen to them when they grew up? Not all kids in that place grow to be adults who marry and live out a controlled, peaceful life. Some have terrible endings way before their time."

"Tell me how should it be."

"Love is special. It's a bond between two people that no one else can break. It's an overwhelming feeling, wanting to do anything and everything to make that person happy." I sigh. "Women like your mum were seen as important. Women like my mum were just breeding machines. They chose the girls they wanted to take and let the rest slave for them. That shouldn't exist in this day and age. Women aren't lesser beings. We're all equal."

"I'd like to leave the bedroom tomorrow," she says, resting her head on my shoulder. It's her way of telling me she's heard enough.

"Okay."

The following day, we head down for breakfast. It's the best way to introduce her to everyone in one go.

It's crazy in the kitchen with everyone shouting and fighting for pancakes. Diamond smiles, giving me a wink. "Take a seat and I'll bring yours over."

Rylee pulls out the seat beside her, and I direct Six to sit down. "How are you?" she asks, and Six shrugs. "It's a mess," says Rylee, "but you'll get through it. We'll help." And in that moment, I love Rylee even more because I know she'll make it her mission to help.

"Is it always like this?" asks Six, and I nod, thanking Diamond as she passes me a plate of fresh pancakes.

"Did you eat breakfast as a family?" asks Rylee, and Six's smile falters. "Sorry, I wasn't thinking."

"It's fine. Yes, sometimes, and we always had dinner together."

"That's nice."

"Not really. We weren't allowed to speak unless spoken to, and I would often get hit if I didn't sit straight."

Rylee arches a brow. "Well, that won't happen here, so slouch away."

After we've eaten, Rylee offers to take Six and introduce her to everyone and show her around, so I head into church for a quick debrief about last night.

"When are we gonna end this idiot?" asks Tatts.

"Good question," says Grim, turning to me and arching his brow.

"We're gonna bring him back here first," I say. "He doesn't deserve a quick death."

"He'll know we're coming," Mav points out.

"We'll lie low for a few days. He's got too much to worry about to think about us. I did checks on the name you gave me," says Ghost. "Turns out, he's the tycoon who owns the village they're staying in."

Grim mutters, "Bet he isn't charging rent."

"One virgin for free living," I add.

"Dice, what are your thoughts on all this? We could've ended him by now, and I know I said I'd let you lead, but it's taking too long," says Mav.

I grip the dice in my hand tightly. "It's not the time," I tell him. He stares at me impatiently, and I know he wants to challenge me. Instead, he sighs, nodding his head.

"Come on, Pres, you can't be serious," snaps Grim, outraged.

"It's Dice's call."

"We all know he's dragging this out for revenge," he argues.

"So what," snaps Mav. "Doesn't he deserve it after everything?"

"Of course, but women are at risk," Grim replies.

I roll the dice, getting everyone's attention. They bounce against Mav's arm and stop. He glances at them and says, "Double six."

I grin before announcing, "Then tonight is the night."

After church, I find Astraea sitting on a couch in the main room, staring into space. I join her and ask, "You okay?"

She nods. "Rylee had to go to work," she says. "I'm not sure where everyone else went."

"Sorry about breakfast. It gets crazy in there."

"It was nice," she says with a small smile. "The chaos distracted me."

"Why don't we go for a walk? There's a field out back." I take her hand and lead her out.

After a few silent minutes, she sighs. "I'm so confused."

"Understandable."

"Why did you take so long to find me?"

"I needed courage to come back. I was a kid, and I was scared. When Diamond found me, I locked a lot of it away, and by the time I found the strength to come back, The Circle had gone."

"Do you see your real dad?"

I shake my head. "I couldn't find him. I guess he left after Mum sent him away. She was scared and knew the Lords wouldn't let her leave willingly. In the end, they killed her in the worst possible way."

"So, she wasn't a sacrifice?"

I stop and turn Astraea to face me. "Six, none of those women were sacrificed. It's not a thing. They tell you that to make you feel special, but it's just murder. Plain and simple."

She shakes her head. "I don't understand any of it. Why would they do that?"

"My mum grew up in care. It meant she had no one, not really, so they preyed on her because they knew no one would come looking. It's how they got a lot of the girls. But when they realised Mum had betrayed them, they decided they'd never risk outsiders coming into their cult ever again. So, they chose who would breed for them. It meant the Lords would get those women pregnant, and if they had girls, they'd be sacrificed, and if they had boys, they'd be raised as disciples. It kept The Circle going for generations. Occasionally, when a girl was born to a Lord, they'd raise her to believe she was important, more important than the rest. She would be trained to be the perfect sacrifice while others would be raised to be good wives to other Lords."

"How would they decide who would marry a Lord and who would be sacrificed?"

I lower to sit on the grass, tugging her to sit too. I take both her hands in my own and examine how tiny they are compared to mine. "I'm not sure. I have a theory, but it's not a good one."

"None of this is good," she points out.

"I think it depends on whether the Lord wanted to have sex with his daughter. Sex meant sacrifice. If he didn't want that, she would marry a Lord." Astraea stares at me for a long time, a range of emotions passing over her face. "I might be wrong," I add.

"What if you are wrong?" she whispers. "What if you're wrong about it all?"

"I wish I was, Six. In the real world, women are free to do what they want. They marry, they love, they have kids who grow up to be safe. They don't get killed or have their kids taken from them. Did you have a choice . . . in any of it?"

"You don't know that they were going to kill me. I was going to meet a man. They were training me to be a good wife."

"He was going to kill you, Astraea."

"You don't know that."

"I do," I hiss through gritted teeth. "They were going to train you. Do you know what that entails? Weeks of fear, making you so terrified that you'll comply. The village they're staying in is owned by a very rich man, and that man had his sights on you. The Circle is living rent free in exchange for you. The whole thing is fucked up, but you better believe they were going to end you."

She's silently sobbing, but her hands remain in mine. "Why didn't they kill you, if they were so worried you'd tell someone?"

"I ran before they could. My mum warned me to run the second I got the chance."

"How do you know for sure they killed her? Maybe they just sent her away?"

"Because I saw it, Astraea. I saw what they did. That's when I realised the truth. The Lords are very sick men with an unhealthy appetite for power, violence, and sex. They spout bullshit about god's will to ease their conscience. And who would know what really went on? Who checks up on the kids there? They don't allow outsiders in, and that's because the children aren't registered anywhere in the world. If I had a child, I'd register the birth so the government knows there's a child born. You have to do that legally. From the minute a woman gets pregnant here, she's checked on by doctors and midwives. That doesn't happen in The Circle. The other women look after the pregnant ones, and they have a doctor living amongst them so no one needs to leave the village."

She pushes to stand. "I need some time alone."

"I can't leave you out here alone," I mutter.

"What happens next?" she asks.

"I don't know. I didn't think about the future. My only goal was to save you."

She folds her arms across her chest and turns back towards the clubhouse. "Maybe I didn't want to be saved," she mutters, walking away.

ASTRAEA

I knock lightly on Cam's door, and he opens it, glancing down the hallway nervously. "Does Malachi know you're here?"

"He doesn't like that name," I remind him, pushing past to go inside.

"Maybe he should be here too."

"Why? I thought we were friends?"

"We are, Rae, but I don't know how much I can share with you, and I'm sure you have many questions."

"You can share everything, because I deserve that after what you did."

"I never planned any of this, Rae. When he approached me, I thought . . . well, it doesn't matter, but he got me tied up and threatened to chop off my fingers unless I brought you to him."

"And you didn't think to question why? You were gonna throw me under the bus?"

"No, it wasn't like that. I knew he'd help, and I'd just learned of your father's plans. I didn't want to lose you, Rae, not like that. I was desperate, and desperate enough to turn to who I thought was a complete stranger because I just wanted to get you out of The Circle."

"Tell me about my father's plans."

He looks down at the floor. "Just know that everything Dice is saying is true."

"So, why did you stick around? You could have left anytime if things were so terrible there."

Cam begins to cry, something I've never seen before, and my heart aches to reach out and hold him. "Because I didn't want to leave you. We talked about it once, about running away. It was after Malachi disappeared and we were confused. Your father overheard, and after that, he made sure I didn't speak of that sort of thing again."

"How?"

Cam fidgets uncomfortably. "He punished me . . . a lot."

"By beating you? I never saw bruises," I say accusingly.

He shakes his head, a sad expression on his face. "No, Rae. He didn't beat me. He . . . he forced me to . . . he forced himself on me."

I eye him suspiciously. "No . . . why would he do that?" It's all too much to take in, and I stand, backing away from him and reaching for the door. "I don't know why you're lying, Cam. I don't understand."

"I'm not," he mutters, swiping his tears away.

I step into the hallway and inhale sharply. The pain in my chest is so intense, I clutch my hand over it. "Everything okay?" I spin to find Rosey watching me cautiously. "Should I get Dice?" I shake my head.

"You want me to take you to your room?" I nod, and she gently takes me by the elbow, leading me away from Cam's room.

I'm relieved to find my own room empty. I don't need to hear anything else to mess my head up, it feels ready to explode. Rosey walks around the room, occasionally stopping to look at a picture or a plant. Dice keeps bringing things to make the room more homely, but he'll never understand that I can't see this as my home. "It must be hard," she eventually says. "It's a lot to take in."

"I don't know what to believe," I admit. "They're asking me to believe my entire life was a lie."

"Dice isn't a liar," she says, sitting on the chair by the window and propping her feet up on the end of the bed. "If he's gone to all this trouble to help you, it's because he's saving you from something or someone."

"I didn't need to be saved."

"How do you know?"

"Because I know my father. He wouldn't do half the things they keep saying."

"I don't think anyone truly knows someone. Everyone has secrets."

"My father is a strict man. He likes things to be perfect, but he's not a . . . he wouldn't hurt me."

"So, he's never hurt you? Not once? He's never hit you or made you feel less than?"

I bite my lower lip, thinking of the times I had cried in my room after he taught me a lesson. "Only for my own good."

"What does that mean?"

"He'd only hit me when I deserved it."

Rosey laughs. "When does anyone deserve to be hit?"

"If I forgot my manners or dinner wasn't ready on time. He just wanted me to be a good wife to someone one day."

"Wow. You really believe that, don't you?"

"It was my job to be a good woman, to make men happy."

Rosey stares through wide, shocked eyes. "Who made you happy, Astraea?"

I think over her question. "I was happy . . . I think."

"Is it so hard to believe your father hurt people? If you really think about everything he ever did or said?"

"Maybe not, but it was my life, it's all I know. Trust me, being here is so much scarier than being there."

"Because it's new, it's going to be. But with time, you'll see that you're better off out of that place." She heads for the door. "It's funny how Josephine has a totally different view to yours, yet you came from the same place."

I sit up straighter. "Josephine?"

"Yeah, the girl Dice saved last night. One of seven, actually. She's really grateful."

CHAPTER NINE

DICE

It's the night I've been waiting for since I was thirteen years old. My brothers are just as pumped as me, but as we pull up onto the side street near The Circle's village, something feels different. The church, which can be seen from here, isn't lit up like usual. We dismount and head towards it. The fence panel, which is usually left ajar, is sealed off. I glance at Mav. "They're gone," I say, dread filling my stomach.

"No way. They can't be." He kicks the fence panel, and it crumbles, giving us access. The church door is open, but there are no lights inside.

"Be careful. I don't like this," I whisper as Mav steps inside cautiously.

"Jesus, it s-s-stinks," complains Scar, covering his mouth and nose.

"Yeah, there's only one stench that gets to the back of your throat like that," mutters Copper.

Maverick flicks on the torch light from his mobile phone. "Fuck," he hisses.

There are three dead bodies on the altar, and when we get closer, we realise they're all young girls. The brothers immediately remove their hoods and lower their heads, all silently praying we catch the bastards before there are any more deaths. "We missed them," I mutter, crouching down and holding my head in my hands. "It's my fault."

Mav pats me on the back. "This isn't on you, brother. It's on those crazy bastards."

A few of the brothers move out to check the village, but I know they've gone. I can feel it. "We're gonna have to call this in," says Mav. "I can't leave these girls to be discovered. We'll do an anonymous call to the police."

When the brothers return and confirm my suspicions, that The Circle have moved on, a rage fills me. "I gotta get out of here," I snap. "I need to clear my head."

My glass is empty, so I hold it out for another refill. The barmaid smiles, filling it halfway. "Are you gonna tell me what's bothering you, biker? You've almost killed a bottle of Jack in the last two hours. I don't wanna have to take your arse to the hospital and get your stomach pumped."

"You ain't gotta worry about me, I've got a stomach of steel," I mutter as she drops some ice into my glass.

She leans over the bar, pushing her tits together until my eyes are only focussed on them. "I like a man who can handle his drink."

"Yeah? I like a woman who can handle a drunk man."

She grins, a glint in her green eyes sparkling. "I get off in an hour, then I'll show you just how good I can be at handling a man." She goes off to serve another customer, and I watch the sway of her tight arse.

My mobile buzzes and I stare at Maverick's name before cancelling the call like I did the last five times. He leaves another message that I don't listen to. Bar girl saunters back over to top up my glass. "Is that the wife," she asks, nodding towards my phone, "wondering where her man is?"

"What if it is?" I ask.

She leans across, grabbing my shirt in her fist and planting her plump lips against mine. "I ain't got loyalty to your wife. If you were mine, I wouldn't let you out of my sight," she whispers against my mouth. My cock strains in my jeans. "I'm gonna show you the best night of your life, and you might never go back to her." She plants another steamy kiss on me before wandering off again to serve someone else.

"Jeeeeeez, you know she's gonna fuck you good but leave you with an STD that'll probably rot your cock," comes Rosey's voice. I groan, briefly closing my eyes in irritation. "Yah know, there're safer options out there."

"What the fuck do you want, Rosey?" I snap.

"I was passing."

"No, you weren't passing. Did Mav send you? I just want some damn peace."

Rosey clicks her fingers to get the barmaid's attention. She looks mildly irritated but comes over. "What can I get you?"

"Vodka, neat."

"Ice?"

"Neat, are you stupid?"

"Rosey," I groan, "don't be a dick."

"I just walked in to see her tongue down your throat," snaps Rosey, and I frown in confusion. "Bitch coming on to my man like I don't know how the fuck to please him."

I sigh heavily. "Don't do that."

"You're the wife?" asks the barmaid, smirking.

"Yeah, I'm the wife. You're lucky I like to watch." The barmaid screws her face up in disgust.

"She isn't my wife," I say, but she's already walking away. "You cockblocked me!" I snap.

"I saved you from knob rot, so you should thank me. Anyway, Mav wants you to come back to the club."

"I was ignoring him for a reason."

"Yeah, I know, you blame yourself for the dead virgins, blah blah blah. Just get back or he said he'll come and get you, and that won't end well for either of you."

"Do you have any compassion?"

"Not really. Something's missing inside of me, I'm aware it's not normal. Would it help if I told you Astraea's gone a little crazy?"

I stare at her. "What . . . why? Is she okay?"

"She demanded we let her see Josephine."

I stand, draining my drink. "How does she know about her?"

Rosey shrugs innocently. "I have no idea."

ASTRAEA

Josephine looks sick. She's pale, with red marks under her eyes, her hair is lank, and there are bruises on her face, wrists, and ankles. She sits in the corner of her room, staring at me. "I'm Astraea," I say quietly.

"I know who you are." She doesn't look happy about that.

"How?"

"We all knew you. The men would talk about the great Astraea, virgin goddess, innocent and pure."

"Why would they talk about me?"

She stares at me like I'm stupid, and I shift uncomfortably. "You begged Maverick to let you in here, so what do you want?"

"I feel like you hate me, yet I don't know you."

"Why would you know me? I'm nothing, no one."

"Rosey told me that Dice rescued you?"

She nods, a small smile playing on her lips. She clearly likes Dice and that doesn't sit well with me. "If it wasn't for him, I'd be dead."

"You were a sacrifice?"

"That's what they told themselves so they could sleep easier."

"Who?"

"You know who. Why are you in here questioning me?" she snaps angrily.

"I . . . I'm confused . . . about The Circle. I don't understand it."

"That's because you were protected in your ivory tower, like a princess. The ultimate prize. But in the end, you were no different from us. You just lived better."

"Where did you live?"

"In the hostel with my mother. It's a side you probably didn't get to see very often, or maybe you knew all along, just like your mother, and you turned a blind eye."

"I didn't know," I say, shaking my head. "I knew there was a place housing mothers and babies."

"A factory," she spits, and I frown. "That's what we likened it to, a never-ending baby factory. Men would visit, day and night. It was constant for our mothers. They didn't get a break."

"Men?" I repeat, and she rolls her eyes in irritation.

"You really have no clue, do you? How the hell do you live for as long as you and be so blind? The factory was like one massive orgy, men coming at all hours to have sex with the women. They'd produce babies—girls like me were raised for sacrifice and boys would become disciples. I was literally alive just so they could kill me."

I wipe the tears running silently down my face. "And my father?"

"Was the Lord of all Lords. The kingpin of it all."

There's a loud banging on the door, and I jump in fright. "Six, open the door," yells Dice.

"How does it feel?" asks Josephine, tipping her head to one side, giving me a look full of hatred. "To have men falling at your feet? They only want you for one thing. We were born to die, but you were born to please."

"No," I whisper, shaking my head.

"Astraea, let me in," he yells.

"Men look at you and want you. They want to be the first man to fuck you and the only man to break you. That's what daddy had planned for his beautiful daughter."

"No," I whisper.

"Yes! He had big plans for you, but you had to ruin it all, and because of you, we had to pay the price."

"Six, now!" The door crashes open and Dice glares between us. "What have you said?" he asks Josephine.

"The truth."

"Six," he mutters, his expression full of regret.

"Where have you been?" I cry, angry he didn't come back to me tonight. If he had, I wouldn't be in here listening to this.

I shove past him, and he almost stumbles back. "She needed to know," I hear her tell him.

I run downstairs and into the main room where a group of bikers sit chatting. "I don't want to be a virgin anymore," I announce, and one of the men spits his beer out in surprise. They all stare wide-eyed.

"Mav, you should get out here," yells one.

Maverick comes out of his office and approaches me warily. "Everything okay? Dice is back now."

"I don't want to be a virgin anymore," I repeat. "Without that, no one would be interested, right?"

Mav smirks. "Maybe that's a discussion you should have with Dice."

I shake my head. "No, it's what he wants too. It's all he wants. Please, someone just help me," I cry, staring at the men.

"I mean, if she really needs to . . ." says one of the men, grinning.

"Not funny, Tatts," snaps Mav, and another of the men slap him upside the head.

I rush over to the large man covered in tattoos from head to toe. "I need to have sex," I say, grabbing his hand.

He stares past me. "It's not how it looks, brother. I was kidding," he says to someone behind me.

I feel Dice's presence but keep hold of the biker's hand. "Please," I whisper, "I won't give you any trouble."

"Shit, brother, she's begging me," he says, a pleading tone in his voice.

"Do you have any idea what I've seen tonight, Six?" growls Dice, still behind me.

"Isn't my virginity the problem?" I yell, releasing my hold on his brother and spinning to face him. "That's the reason they want me back, right? The reason you took me, right? So, if I get rid of it, no one will want me, and I'll be left alone."

"That's not why I took you," he snaps.

"Men, let's fall out and leave them to it," orders Mav. The brothers file out, and then we're alone.

"Why did you take me?"

"I am nothing like them," he spits through gritted teeth.

"Don't pretend you haven't thought about it," I yell.

"Not like that," he yells back. "I'd never hurt you or do anything you don't want to."

"Yah know what, just take it. Save us all the hassle," I shout, yanking my top off over my head and throwing it to the floor.

"Jesus," he snaps, grabbing it and trying to wrestle me back into it. "Put your clothes on."

"It's what you want. It's what all men want from me. I don't know who to trust."

He bends slightly, and then I'm upside down and he's marching up the stairs with me over his shoulder. He dumps me on my bed and throws my top at me. "Tonight, I went back to The Circle," he growls. I sit slightly, wondering if he saw my mother. "Yah know what I found?" I shake my head. "Dead bodies. Three girls, no older than twenty, naked, with their throats cut." I gasp, sadness filling my heart. "And it's my fault." I get to my feet and reach up to touch his face, but he steps back from me and my hand falls to my side. "I was so busy wanting revenge, hoping to drag out the deaths of those fuckers, that I lost sight of everything else. I was close enough to kill your father, twice. Twice! And I let him walk away. I was so obsessed with causing him fear before I took him out, I didn't think about the girls he'd hurt."

"You wanted revenge for your mum?" I whisper.

"And for you," he says. "For what they did and what they were going to do to you. He knew all along, yah know. He knew we were meant to be. He once told me that everyone could see our connection, and in a different life, we'd have it all, but your destiny was already set in the stars. He promised me, when the time was right, he'd let me join the Lords. And I knew . . . I knew I had to get you out of there, but then it all went to shit and they left. I spent years thinking about you, and seeing you again was like a second chance. But I failed, because they've left again and I don't know where they are. They could turn up anytime and take you back, and fuck knows how many girls will die now."

My heart beats faster. "Then take it," I whisper, grabbing his hand, and he lets me. "Take what they want so badly."

He shakes his head. "No. That doesn't solve anything. They'll still send you to your death at the hands of some crazed millionaire."

I guide his hand to my shoulder, and he watches. "But even if they do, they won't get to take this from me. Shouldn't I get to choose?"

"Yes, but not like this," he mutters as I guide his hand to drag my bra strap from my shoulder.

"Show me what it's supposed to be like," I murmur, dragging his fingers across my chest to the other strap. I leave his hand at the swell of my breast. "Please."

A strangled sound leaves his throat. He's fighting with himself, and I know exactly how to help him. I reach into his pocket, gasping when my hand brushes his hard penis. I pull out the dice and cup my hands around them, gently shaking them. He takes my wrist, closing his eyes and blowing on them, and when he opens them and releases me, I throw the dice to the floor. They bounce before landing on a double two. He growls. It's deep and sends a shiver down my spine. Then, he slams his mouth against mine, kissing me. He pulls my bra down to my waist, exposing my breasts, and rubs his thumbs over my erect nipples. I gasp as the sensation warms my insides.

He walks me back until my legs hit the bed. Guiding me to lie down, he lays beside me, propping his head on his hand and using his free hand to run up and down my stomach. He lowers his head, keeping his eyes fixed to mine as he runs his tongue over one of my nipples.

DICE

Astraea looks so beautiful lying beside me, watching me through her innocent eyes. Every touch or kiss makes her gasp aloud, and fuck, it's a turn-on. Everything in me wants to sink into her, but I have to take it slow.

I peel her jeans down her legs, placing gentle kisses as I work my way back to her soft lips. We kiss, and I trail my hand back over her stomach and to her thigh, where I draw small invisible circles over her skin. As I move my hand to her inner thigh, her legs fall open. "Anytime you want me to stop, you just say the words. I won't be mad. This is all your choice," I tell her, and she nods. "I need to hear the words, Six."

"Okay."

"If something feels good and you want me to keep doing it, just say."

"Okay."

I go back to kissing her and exploring her skin with my fingers. I trace over the material of her cotton underwear, and her body jerks in response. "That feel good, Six?" I whisper, and she nods shyly. I repeat the move, and her lip's part, inviting me for another kiss. I move my hand under the material. "Is this okay?" She nods again, and as I part her with my fingers, wetness drips out. "And this?" She nods, biting her lower lip when I run my finger through the wetness and hum my approval.

I make sure my finger is coated in her juices before I slide it over her swollen clit. Her hands grab hold of my shoulders, and her eyes widen in surprise. "Relax," I whisper, doing it again. Her toes curl, and she grips tighter with each circle. I suck her nipple into my mouth, and she whimpers, squeezing her eyes closed.

I remove my hand and her eyes shoot open. "I'm not going anywhere," I reassure her, rolling over to kneel between her legs. Her scent hits me, and I stare at the wet patch on her underwear. "You're so beautiful," I whisper, running my eyes up her body until they meet hers. She smiles shyly. I remove her underwear and lay between her legs, my face level with her most intermate place. I part her using my thumbs. "Remember, you can stop anytime," I remind her.

I lick her, running my tongue from the back of her opening to the front in one fluid motion. She quivers, fisting the sheets. Her taste is addictive, and I close my mouth over her, paying the most attention to her sensitive clit. I hook my hands around her thighs, holding her in place as I taste her. She occasionally jerks, throwing her arm over her eyes, then her hands go to my hair, pushing me closer as she rubs herself against my mouth. I push my finger into her opening, and it sends her spiralling through an orgasm.

CHAPTER TEN

ASTRAEA

I can't quite catch my breath. My entire body is shaking uncontrollably as a warm feeling works its way from the tips of my toes upwards until I'm certain I'm glowing. Dice doesn't stop licking me until the shaking subsides and tears are leaking from the corners of my eyes. When he crawls up my body, the bulge in his jeans is obvious. He smiles down at me, his mouth and beard damp from my arousal, and I feel myself blush with embarrassment.

"That was the most amazing experience of my life," he tells me, kissing me. I taste myself on him and turn my head. He grins, gripping my chin and holding me in place while he kisses me. "You taste fucking amazing, so don't be embarrassed. Let's shower."

He stands, tugging me up. "But we haven't . . ." I trail off, too embarrassed to say the words aloud.

"One step at a time," he says, leading me to the bathroom, where he turns on the shower. He kicks off his jeans, his bulge still protruding from his boxer shorts. Leaving his shorts and T-shirt on, he gently pushes me into the shower. He follows, his clothes instantly soaking to his skin.

I watch as he lathers a sponge with a shower gel Rylee gave me. He wets it until it foams and then begins to slide it over my shoulders and neck. "Are you okay?" he asks. I nod, and he grins. "You've done a lot of nodding but not much talking, Six."

"I don't know what to say," I admit. A part of me is wondering why he didn't go all the way, why he stopped without taking his own pleasure. The other part is reeling from my first ever sexual experience. It felt good, so good I wanted him to carry on.

"Did you enjoy it?"

"Yes." I'm conflicted, knowing those things should only happen in marriage but desperately wanting him to do it all again, and I can't say any of that out loud without shame washing over me.

"It isn't wrong," he tells me, like he's read my mind, and I look at the soapy water escaping down the drain.

"We're not married."

"You want us to be? I can sort that." He grins when I look up at him in shock.

I laugh nervously. "No. No. God, no."

"Way to make a guy feel good," he says, his smile fading to awkward.

"How many times have you . . . done that?"

He runs the sponge over my breasts and that same warm tingling sensation returns, hitting me hard. "Does it matter?" The sponge trails down until he rubs between my legs, and I gasp.

His erection is still standing at attention and guilt hits me. I'm supposed to please him, and I don't feel like I have at all. He watches me cautiously as I remove the sponge from his grasp. "I should wash you," I explain.

I wait patiently while he lifts his wet shirt and drops it to the floor. I stare down at his shorts, waiting for him to remove them. After a few silent seconds, he pushes them down his legs and kicks them to one side. I stare at his manhood. It's not the first time I've seen one, but it's the first time I've ever felt a desire to touch it.

I wipe the sponge over his chest, moving around until I'm behind him. I lather the soap like an expert, rubbing small circles over his body until he's covered, then I move back to his front and lower to my knees. He watches me through hooded eyes as I squeeze the sponge over his erection, mesmerized by the soap suds running down his shaft. I drop the sponge and wrap my hands around him. He inhales sharply, and I massage the soap into him, occasionally cupping his balls. "Would you like me to clean you with my mouth?" I ask robotically.

When he doesn't reply, I look up, and he's staring down at me with horror. His penis deflates, and he hooks his hands under my arms and lifts me to stand. "Rinse off," he says sharply. Stepping past me, he gets out of the shower and wraps himself in a towel. He grabs me one, holding it out, and when I step from the shower, he wraps me up. "Are you hungry? I can get you something."

I shake my head, wondering why he's suddenly so cold. "Did I do something wrong?" I ask.

His silence speaks volumes, and then he forces a smile. "Of course not," he lies. "Everything's fine."

"But I didn't please you," I say, pointing to his crotch area.

"You don't need to."

"My father said it's my job to—"

"Ignore everything he said. It's wrong. All of it," he suddenly snaps, causing me to flinch. He bites his lower lip and looks at the ground. He does that whenever he's trying to keep calm. "I'll get you something to eat. Rest."

Dice snatches his wet clothes from the floor and leaves. I stare at the closed door, unable to stop the tears. I don't like that I made him angry. Maybe my father was right. I'll never be good enough to be a wife. I don't even know how to please a man.

DICE

I sit at the kitchen counter, rolling the dice over and over. Each time, I get even numbers. I growl, snatching them up as Rosey skips in. She comes to a stop, and I feel her eyes assess my half-naked body. "Who knew you were hiding all that," she says, grinning with approval. "How much for you to drop the towel?"

I roll my eyes. "Go away."

"You use that line a lot with me," she points out, taking a seat beside me. "One day, I might take offence. What's wrong?"

"Why do you always show up when—"

"When you need me? I'm so in tune with you."

I laugh, because it's hard not to when she's so persistent. "I just had a harsh reminder of The Circle," I tell her.

"Did it involve Rae being naked too?" she asks, arching a brow, and I nod. "Did you—"

"No, I wasn't gonna take it that far today. She needs time and patience."

"It'll take a while for The Circle to get out of her head completely."

I scrub my hands over my face. "How did you move on . . . yah know, after what Eagle did to you?"

She shrugs, shifting uncomfortably. Our last president, Mav's dad, wasn't a good man, and he hurt

Rosey, getting her pregnant with Mav's half-brother, Ollie. "I'm not sure I have," she mutters. "I went down a destructive path, one I'm still on, I think. But sex, that came easy. It's just sex. The emotions are what I can't deal with. I always feel like . . . well, like I'm not worthy, yah know?"

"To be loved?"

"I guess. Some part of me still feels dirty and used. If I'm the one using men, it's easier to deal with and I'm in control. At least, that's what my therapist tells me."

"You have therapy?" I ask, my turn to arch a brow.

She laughs. "Yep, imagine how crazy I'd be without it."

She stands, almost pressing into my side, then I feel her mouth near my ear. "If you ever wanna burn off some of that worry, I'm good at the no-strings part," she whispers, kissing me on the cheek and leaving me alone.

I make one of the club girls take Six a snack and I head to my own room. Tonight was beautiful, something I've never experienced before. But seeing her like that, so robotic and compliant, brought me crashing from my lust-filled bubble. She's damaged, broken, and having sex with her won't make anything better. In fact, I feel like I took advantage of her, and now, I'm ashamed.

I'm lying on my bed, staring up at the ceiling when there's a knock at my door. Jo peers around the door, smiling when she sees me. "You okay?" I ask.

She comes in, leaving the door open, and sits on the edge of my bed. "I hope I didn't make things worse with Astraea."

"It's fine. Like you said, she needs to know the truth. We were taking it slow, trying to unpick her gently. That's what the therapist suggested. If we flood her with bad shit, it might send her over the edge."

"She's spent her whole life being protected," she mutters. I know how she must view Astraea. It was tough being in the lower ranks, where the Lords and their families were seen as better and more deserving. We were literally there to please them.

"Did Rylee talk to you about getting you back on your feet?"

She nods. "It's scary, yah know. I don't know how to live alone without decisions being made for me."

I smile. "We're not gonna kick you out and leave you to it. Rylee knows people who can help you through every step, and you'll always have the club to come back to when you need us."

"Is that what will happen with her?"

"Astraea?"

She nods. "Will she go into the big bad world alone?"

I hadn't thought about it until earlier. It's another reason I can't have sex with her. Deep down, she deserves freedom, and if I have sex with her, I won't want to let her go. I've spent my life loving her, even when she wasn't with me. My feelings are too powerful to ignore, and sealing that will make it worse. "Eventually."

"Really?" She looks surprised.

"You all deserve to be free."

"What if I don't want that?" she asks, biting her lower lip. I watch as she places her hand over my chest, trailing her finger over one of the tattoos there. "What if I want to stay here, with you?"

I stare wide-eyed. What the fuck am I giving off tonight to make these women behave like this around me? "Jo, you need to live a life where you're free to do exactly what you want when you want. This life, it's not for you."

"You don't know that. Maybe I like to be controlled." Her hand moves lower until she's tugging the towel open.

"Jo, come on, this isn't what you want. You don't even know me." She grips my cock, and it begins to harden. I take her wrist, but she grips tighter. "Please," I mutter. "I don't know you, and you've had a lot of shit to deal with. This isn't what you want."

"I owe you so much," she whispers. "You saved me."

"I'm trying to let you down gently here, but you're not listening to me." Her hand moves, and I groan. "Jo, stop!" I snap.

"No one needs to know," she says, rubbing her thumb over the tip of my erection and smoothing the precum over the head. She releases me to pop the digit into her mouth. "You taste good," she whispers, smirking. I snatch her wrist before she can grab me again. There's something different about her—she's not shy or scared like Astraea and it makes me suspicious.

Movement by the door catches my eye, and I see the horrified look on Six's face right before she runs away. "Fuck," I snap, shoving Jo away from me and wrapping my towel back in place.

ASTRAEA

I lock my door right as Dice reaches it, and he slams his hands against it. "Six, please, that's not what it looked like."

I slide down the door, clutching my chest where my heart beats rapidly. *Why does it hurt?* I've seen men use women over and over. My brother was always bringing women back to the house, even when his wife was there. I saw the hurt on my sister-in-law's face and wondered why she cared. Because if the men were happy, we could live in peace.

But with Dice, it's different. My feelings towards him are growing. He took me from everything I knew, yet he's treated me so nice and been so patient, and I was starting to believe what he said about The Circle and the evil that runs through it. But it turns out, he's no different. He's driven by sex, by dark desires, just like the men in The Circle.

"Astraea, please, you have to believe me. *Fuck*, tonight's been crazy."

"I thought you didn't want sex," I mutter. "But it was just with me you didn't want it?"

"No, Six, that's not it."

"She knows what to do," I say. "She's better at it."

"Fuck, Six, open the door so we can talk."

"I'd like to go home now," I whisper, wiping my wet cheeks with the back of my hand.

"No, don't say that, Rae. You don't want to go back there. Jo is confused. She doesn't want to have sex with me, she's just unsure of everything, a bit like you."

"So, you were helping her, like you did me?" Somehow, that stings more. How many others is he helping?

"No. She came on to me, she touched me. I didn't want her to."

"I heard what you said," I admit, "that one day you'll set me free."

"If that's what you want."

I nod, even though he can't see me. "Yes. It is. I'd like to go now."

"Not now, Six. You're not ready yet."

"Because I'm still a virgin?"

"No. Fuck, it's not about that."

"You can still take it, if that's what you want. It's more important to you than me."

"I don't want to have sex with you," he snaps, and my heart takes another hit. I hear his intake of breath, and he slowly releases it. "I didn't mean it like that," he adds, more softly this time. It confirms what Father told me—I'd never be good enough without training.

"I don't want to see you again," I say, rubbing my hand over the pain in my chest. "Rylee can help me."

"You're just saying that because I hurt you," he mutters. "I didn't mean to. Truth is, Six, there's been no one but you. Not ever. I've loved you since I was a kid."

I place my hand against the door and sob quietly. "Things changed after you left," I whisper. "And now I've grown up, I don't see you like that." My heart twists with each word. "I don't want to see you again, Dice."

"Open the door, Six. I want you to look me in the eye and say it," he snaps.

I pull myself to stand, taking a deep breath and holding it until I open the door and I'm face to face with him. His stance is angry as he glares at me, like he's challenging me to say the words but thinking I won't. "I don't want to see you again," I repeat, staring hard into his eyes. His hand goes into my hair and he pushes me back a few steps. His eyes are so full of pain, it almost chokes me.

"You don't fucking mean that, Rae. You let me touch you, taste you . . . you wanted me."

"I just wanted you to take my virginity. It was a means to an end."

"Bullshit. You're lying."

I don't flinch, keeping my face cold and blank. I'd learned long ago how to shut my emotions down. "I don't like you in that way, Malachi."

He releases me. "Then why didn't you let me fuck Jo? Why did you run off and lock yourself away?"

I shrug. "Shock that you'd move onto her in the same night."

"So, I can go and fuck her right now, and you wouldn't care?" he snaps, and I shake my head. "You're lying."

"Maybe you could show me how to be good at it. I can watch."

He slams his hand into the wall and the plaster cracks. I step back from him and lower my eyes, like I would when my father got angry. Somehow, if I avoided eye contact, it would calm him. "You're lying, Six. I hurt you, and I'm sorry. I don't want her or anyone else. Just you. I didn't push for sex tonight because I want to take it slow. I don't want to rush you. I care because I love you. What you saw and heard was me trying to let Jo down gently without upsetting her."

I've already seen his actions, so his words mean nothing. "I'd like to sleep now," I say, turning away from him.

"I'm not leaving," he says firmly.

I remove my robe. He's already seen me naked, and maybe a small part of me wants him to see what he's missed out on. I saw the way his eyes were full of heat when Josephine touched him like she did, not like when I was on my knees in front of him and he looked horrified. I climb into bed, and he takes a seat by the window. "Thanks for earlier," I mutter, closing my eyes. "It was nice."

CHAPTER ELEVEN

ASTRAEA

I wake to that warm feeling rushing through my body. It takes me a second to realise Dice is between my legs, tasting me again. I struggle, trying to shove his head away, but he grips my thighs, licking harder. "Nice," he snaps. "It was fucking nice?" He's referring to my last comment before I fell asleep, and he doesn't seem happy about it. "I'll show you fucking nice." He pushes his finger into me, and I arch my back off the bed. "Is that nice, Six?" he mutters, inserting another until I feel too full. He begins to thrust them in and out, occasionally sucking me into his mouth.

"You don't think I've thought about this moment my entire fucking adult life? I'd love nothing more than for you to come on my cock, Six. I've dreamt of it. I want to hear you scream my name. I want you smelling of me. I want to make you *mine*," he growls. I cry out as a wave of pleasure rips through me. His dirty mouth is making it so much more intense. "I can do things that'll make you come so hard, but we have to take it slow. I want to show you that sex is about pleasure, for both of us, not just me."

He kneels between my legs, keeping his fingers inside me. He moves them faster, placing his other hand on my stomach to hold me still. His thumb presses against my clit, the friction sending me spiralling out of control. Pulling the pillow over my face, I scream into it as my body convulses. He moves his fingers so fast, my body shakes with his thrusts. And then a sensation washes over me and wetness sprays between my legs. I feel the sheets beneath me soak it up, but I'm unable to shift from it because my muscles feel like mush and I'm too weak to roll away.

Dice drops down beside me. "*Nice*," he mutters, shaking his head. "*Fuck nice.*"

I feel my eyes closing, heavy from exhaustion. I don't bother to pull the sheet over me or move from the dampness.

I open my eyes and slowly look to my left where Dice is still sleeping. My body aches and I wince as I roll onto my side to look at him. He looks peaceful like this, though his brow occasionally twitches, as does his lips. He's still wrapped in the towel he put on after our shower. One leg is laid at an angle, making the towel part slightly but not enough to show what's underneath. I tentatively reach for the fabric's edge, my hand shaking as I lift it to part more. The urge to touch him is strong. His penis is soft, resting against his thigh as I run a finger up his leg and then along his shaft. I glance at him and take him in my hand, feeling the weight. It begins to harden even though he's still sleeping. I move my hand and the skin around the penis moves too. I feel Dice shift, then he opens his eyes and gives me a sleepy smile. Frowning, he looks down to where my hand is still moving. "Six, what are—"

"Shh," I whisper. "I just wanna feel."

He bites on his lower lip before nodding once, then he props his head up using a pillow and watches silently while I touch him. I move my hand faster, and his breathing quickens. It feels different touching Dice, more intimate and special. I get onto my knees and move between his open legs. Gripping his erection with both hands, I continue to move up and down, watching him closely. I like having this control over such a strong man. I feel powerful.

I slow my hands and lower my lips to his shaft. He watches through hooded eyes as I tentatively lick the end of his penis, and I hear his sharp intake of breath. It's all the encouragement I need, so I try again, this time closing my lips over the head. His breathing is heavy and rapid, telling me he enjoys everything I'm doing. I suck him into my mouth, wincing when he touches the back of my throat. "Fuck, Six. You keep this up and I'm gonna explode," he pants, gripping a fistful of bedsheet.

I release him from my mouth and hold him with my hands. "I don't like the taste," I whisper, feeling ashamed to admit I've done this before.

"You don't have to do anything you don't want to, Six," he reassures me.

I go back to working him with both hands wrapped tightly around his erection. He doesn't take his eyes off me. Suddenly, he stiffens, throwing his head back and releasing a guttural sound from the back of his throat. I feel his penis swell and then he ejaculates, coating my hands in his release. I'm turned-on. My breathing matches his, and I feel wetness between my legs. Fidgeting, I try to ease the ache there.

Dice eventually sits up, taking my hands and wiping away his mess using his towel. "Sorry," he mutters, placing a gentle kiss on my forehead.

I move my head until we're looking into each other's eyes. I angle my face until our mouths meet, then I gently swipe my tongue into his mouth, the way he does when he kisses me. He places his hands on my cheeks, pulling back slightly. "Slower," he whispers, and I smile shyly. I've never kissed anyone until him, and he always makes the first move. I try again, slowing it down. I throw my leg over his knee so I'm straddling him, and I feel his penis growing again.

I rub myself against him, and he pulls back again, this time breaking the kiss. "Six," he says, his tone warning. I look down between us, angling my body so his penis is against my vagina. I begin to move again, continuing to rub against him. "Six," he whispers, this time sounding pained.

"I want to," I say, nodding and smiling, trying desperately to convince him.

He grips my hips, stilling me. "It's too soon."

"Please," I murmur as I rock, ignoring the way his fingers dig into my hip bone as he tries to stop me. "I want to."

"Earlier, you couldn't stand the sight of me, and now, you wanna have sex?"

I close my eyes, letting my head fall back as the warm feeling builds in my stomach. "It feels right," I whisper.

He runs his hands up my body, seemingly giving up his argument but making no move to penetrate me. Instead, he allows me to rock against him, helping me to reach my orgasm by pulling me down and taking my nipple in his mouth. "Take what you need, Six, but sex is off the table until you're one hundred percent ready," he whispers. "And I have to tell you, I can't wait to watch you ride my cock like this." His words send me spiralling, and I shudder, enjoying the warmth of my orgasm. "Fuckkk," he growls, his own release squirting over his stomach. I smile, wiping my thumb through his release and rubbing gentle circles until it soaks into his skin. He pulls me to lie beside him, wrapping me into his arms and holding me against him. "Sleep, Six."

DICE

I lie awake with Rae in my arms. It feels right, like she was made to fit beside me, but what I said to Jo earlier was true. I can't keep her here. She deserves her freedom because she's never had it. One day, I'll have to let her go, and the thought terrifies me.

I grab my mobile from the bedside table. Mav's called me and sent a text.

Maverick: We might have a lead. Church at nine a.m.

I check the time—it's almost seven. I slowly ease my arms from around Six until I'm free and then wrap my towel around my waist. I bend to place a kiss on her forehead and then slip from her room and head to my own to shower and change into my running gear.

I've been running a solid hour. My heart is thumping heavy in my chest, and I can hear the blood rushing around my body. I slow until I come to a stop and place my hands on my knees. Fuck, I've pushed myself hard. "I'd know that arse anywhere." I look up, and Rosey is jogging towards me, also dressed in running gear.

"Since when do you run?"

She grins, stopping beside me. "I have to keep in shape for when I'm climbing into windows or chasing down my latest victim."

I sit on the damp grass, and she joins me. I love this time of day, when people are rushing to work, using the park as a cut-through. "I don't know how you do it," I say. "Using those hands to slit the throats of men and then going home to get your son ready for school."

She shrugs. "It's my job."

"It's messed up."

"Men do it all the time. Mav has Ella, and Scar has August and Zane. Grim has Oakley. They take care of business and go home to their kids like nothing's happened."

"It's different," I argue.

"Because I'm a woman?" I can tell by her tone she's offended.

I shrug. "I guess. I dunno, I just feel like it's wrong. Women are meant to be nurturing and kind."

"I'm those things too," she says, smirking.

"I'd want the mother of my kids to depend on me, not go out and take lives like it's nothing."

"I'm not gonna be offended by a guy who rolls dice to determine his next move," she retorts.

"Actually, I haven't done that an awful lot lately. Since Rae, things seem clearer."

Rosey falls back on the grass. "I only kill men who deserve it."

"How do you know they deserve it? Who decides?"

"I get hired and then I do my homework. I don't just take a life without giving it careful consideration."

"What if the person who hires you is lying?"

"That's why I do my homework. I watch, wait, and decide. You can't kill on a whim."

I laugh. "How does that conversation even go? You just get a call out the blue? How do they get your number?"

"Word of mouth, mainly. There aren't many female assassins out there. I have a good reputation."

"So, they just put a call in and give you a sob story?"

"I don't meet the people who hire me. I have an agent who does that."

I glare at her. "An agent?"

"Yeah. It keeps things simple if you have a middle man."

"Let me get this straight. You work for someone?"

"Not really. They kind of work for me. A partnership. Have you never seen *John Wick*?"

"Jesus, it's too early to take all this in. Does Mav know about your agent?"

She shrugs. "I don't know. He's never asked me, so maybe not. It's no big deal. It's just my job."

I push to stand. "Weird," I mutter, shaking my head before running in the direction of the club, with Rosey right behind me.

Everyone is hyped in church. We all want the same thing, means we're all after the smell of blood. Mav points on the map to an abandoned warehouse. "It's a twenty-minute ride out, so really not far. The place has been abandoned for years, but we've had word that there's movement there. I've sent two prospects to hide out and watch. I'll keep everyone up to date."

"How's Rae doing?" Grim asks.

"Getting there," I say, her moans of ecstasy playing on loop in my head.

"Is she likely to run back to them?"

I shake my head. "Therapy seems to be going well, she's got another session today. And Rylee is gonna do some work with her about the outside world and what happens next."

"And what does happen next?" asks Grim.

"The end goal is that she moves on with her life. Away from The Circle. Cam has begun therapy too, and I think it would be a good idea that they both move into sheltered accommodation soon. They need to experience freedom."

I feel the brothers staring at me. "But I thought you and she were—" Mav begins.

"Nah, it ain't like that. She's lost and confused. She deserves to fly free."

"You're gonna do that thing," says Grim, "let her fly and see if she returns?"

I shrug. "Maybe."

"It's a dangerous game, brother," he adds.

"I know, but it wouldn't be fair for me to expect anything of her right now. She hasn't experienced life yet."

Mav dismisses everyone but asks me to stay behind. Grim also remains, and they fix me with a hard stare. "Have you thought about this?" asks Mav. "It's clear you care for the woman."

"I love her, Pres," I admit, "and that's why I have to do this."

"Brother, she'll have her freedom here. You can show her all the things she's missing."

I smirk. "It would be selfish of me to make her stay. And I'd never know if she truly loved me or if she was staying through fear of what's beyond these walls. She needs to see what's out there before she settles down."

Mav gives a nod, glancing at Grim before adding, "Okay, well, I'll get Rylee to set the wheels in motion."

I tap on Six's door. Her therapist is about to arrive, and I want to check she's awake. I push the door and find her sitting on her bed reading a book. She blushes when she sees it's me and places the book down, dragging a pillow over it. I frown, moving closer and reaching under the pillow. "What are you hiding?" I ask, grinning.

She grabs the pillow and buries her embarrassed face into it. "Rosey gave it to me," she wails.

The cover shows a topless man. "Are you reading smut?" I tease.

She falls back onto the bed, keeping her face hidden. "I didn't know it was like that."

I laugh, opening the book randomly. I read a few lines and raise my eyebrows. "Whoa, this shit is . . . damn, is it all like this?" I flick through more pages, lying beside her on the bed. "It's page-to-page smut."

"Stop reading it," she cries, grabbing blindly for the book.

I move it from her reach. "He did what," I gasp in mock horror. "Nobody can do that, Six. At least, not in real life."

"I want the earth to swallow me whole," she mutters, still hiding her face with the pillow.

"Now, this part is a thing," I say, reading with interest. "This gives some good ideas. Did a woman write it?" I ask, turning back to the cover. "Makes sense. This is like a glimpse into a woman's mind," I add. "All men could learn from this."

She slams the pillow down beside her. "Stop, now, I'm so embarrassed."

I laugh, laying the book down. "It's okay to read this sort of thing, Six. Loads of women do."

"I didn't know this sort of thing existed," she says.

"Does it make you feel good reading it?" She blushes deeper, and I grin. "I could always check for myself," I add, winking. I run my hand down between her legs. "Six, you bad, bad girl," I tease, and she makes a grab for the pillow again. I move it away from her and continue to run my fingers through her wetness. "Now, I'd love nothing more than to continue exploring you, but you have a very important date," I say, removing my fingers and staring at the glistening evidence of her arousal. I suck my fingers into my mouth and hum my approval. "You taste of heaven. Now, get dressed before your therapist walks in on me eating you."

Rylee grabs me when I get back downstairs, leaving Six to her therapy session. "Mav said you want me to find Rae somewhere to live?" I nod. "Wouldn't she be better staying here until you know she's not in danger?"

"I thought the places you had set up were safe houses?"

"Well, yeah, they are, but Rae is still very vulnerable. What if they find a way to get to her and talk her into going back?"

"They won't. We can spare a prospect to watch over her, and she'll be with Cam, who will call me if anything suspicious happens." She follows me outside to my bike. "Besides, hopefully, the threat will be gone very soon and she'll be free to live her life."

"She told me," Rylee blurts out, and I turn back to look at her. "That you two have done stuff."

I can't hide the annoyance that Six has talked about us to others. "So?"

"So, don't you think you're making it harder?"

"For who?"

"For both of you, Dice. You're the first man who's ever shown her real affection."

Guilt hits me and I stare down at the ground. "I know you mean well, Rylee, but it's none of your business."

"Actually, it is, as the President's old lady and as your friend," she snaps, placing her hands on her hips. "You should be honest with her."

I take a calming breath. "You're right," I mutter. "I'm being selfish. I'll sort it out." I push my helmet on and throw my leg over my bike. "Thanks for the pep talk."

My mum isn't buried anywhere, as her body no longer exists. The Circle didn't leave any evidence behind when they killed her. Instead, I waited until I was old enough to afford a plaque for her, which I chose to place in the local crematorium.

I lay a single white rose beside the plaque and take a seat. I don't believe in talking to the dead, and I never sit here. Usually, I show up, leave a rose, and go. But today, I need to feel comfort, and there's only ever two women who could give me that—my mum and Six. I rest my elbows on my knees and lower my head. "Mum, what the fuck am I doing?" I ask aloud. "I finally found her, and now, I have to let her go? Why did I bother to track her down if I can't keep her?" I sigh. "I want her to be happy and free, but fuck, I want her to be those things with me."

"She won't answer." I look up and see Rosey staring at me.

"What the fuck?" I snap, standing. "This is becoming too weird."

"Relax," she says, laughing. "I was here visiting Eagle's grave."

"Why would you visit him?"

She shrugs. "To make sure he's still in the ground. To tell him how much I fucking hate him. But mainly, so I can tell him about his son and how amazing he is, no thanks to him."

"If you don't mind, I came here for some peace." I sit back down, groaning when she sits beside me.

"Don't be like that. I'm a good listener. By the way, Jo left today," she says, and I frown.

"I didn't know she was going."

"It was out of the blue, to be honest. Rylee was surprised. She announced she had family and was going to stay with them."

"Her family is The Circle," I say. "She wouldn't know anyone outside of it."

Rosey shrugs. "Ask Rylee, she knows more. How're things with Six?"

"None of your business."

"You slept with her yet?"

"No, Rosey. I'm not a complete arse."

"Hey, no judging here. I've done so much stupid shit in my time, I'm the least qualified to judge you."

The need to discuss things is overwhelming, so I relent, sighing before I admit, "We have done stuff, though—her choice, not mine."

"Yeah, she told me."

I glare at her. "Jesus, has she told everyone?" I snap.

Rosey laughs. "Girls need to talk about that shit. We explode if we don't off-load."

"Is that why you gave her the book?"

She grins. "Does she like it?"

"It's smutty and completely far-fetched."

"That's the point. Fantasy and dreams are all us ladies have to get us through the tough times."

"I don't think she needs those sorts of high expectations."

"Look, if you can't compete, it isn't the book's fault. Don't be hating on my smut."

I take another deep breath, releasing it slowly. "I asked Rylee to find her a place in sheltered accommodation."

Rosey sits straighter. "What? Why?"

"Because I think she'd flourish having her freedom. Yah know, when we were kids, we questioned everything The Circle taught us. That doubt never really left her, she just kept her mouth shut for a quiet life. They're out of her life now, and I want her to experience the life she's been missing."

"She can do that at the club."

"Not if I claim her. She's never had sex, Rosey. She needs to do all the shit she never got to do."

Rosey scoffs. "Random hook-ups and drunken mistakes are not her thing, and they never will be. If you send her out there alone, she'll get into all kinds of bother."

"She won't be alone. She'll still have the club in her life, and me, even if it's just as friends."

"I think you're making a huge mistake, Dice. In fact, roll your shiny gold cubes of wisdom and check."

I grin. "I did that already, several times. It's the right thing to do."

CHAPTER TWELVE

ASTRAEA

Therapy is hard. It tires me out, and so, when I wake in the late afternoon, I'm not surprised. I don't even remember nodding off. I glance at the book Rosey gave me. It's full of sex and I can't deny it's got my interest piqued. I want to try those kinds of things, and I want to try them with Dice. I smile to myself at the thought of him. Seeing him with Josephine hurt my heart, only confirming my true feelings for him. I'd never experienced that before. I haven't experienced a lot of the things he's shown me lately, but I'm enjoying experiencing them with him. He feels safe, like I can be myself around him, something I've not been for a very long time.

I head downstairs. I've never come out of my room alone before, but my nerves soon disappear when I spot Rylee and some of the other women sitting around. Rylee smiles, standing as I approach. "Just the person," she says, taking my hand. "I came to find you after your therapist left, and you were out cold on the bed."

"It exhausts me," I reply.

She leads me away from the others to a quiet corner, and we sit at a table. "So, I thought we could do some work together on preparing you for life after."

"After?"

"Yeah, after here, your next chapter."

"Oh." I hadn't thought about what happens next or where I'd go. I just assumed I'd stay here.

"You have your freedom back, Rae. It's exciting," she says, rubbing my arm.

"I guess. I just feel a little overwhelmed. I've never been alone."

She smiles kindly. "You'll never be alone. Not really. You'll always have the club now, and you have Cam." I notice how she doesn't say Dice and I begin to wonder if this is his idea.

"Have other people gone on to live happy, normal lives?"

"Honestly, I don't know. This is unchartered territory for me. But I'm an expert in women's trauma, and I've helped a lot of women get their lives back on track after suffering terrible ordeals. I have every faith I can do that for you too."

Rylee spends an hour going over some things with me. It's very overwhelming, so when Dice walks in and we make eye contact, I'm drawn to him. I make my excuses to Rylee, thanking her for her time, and rush over to him. "You've been gone all day," I say, wrapping my arms around his waist and pressing my face into his chest. He hesitantly returns the hug. "Rylee is talking about me getting a place, and my therapist wants me to get out more," I rush to tell him. "And honestly, the thought makes me feel sick."

He gives me a sympathetic smile. "How about I help with that?"

My thoughts immediately turn to the way his mouth does wonderful things to my body, and I blush. He grins, grabbing a cap from a nearby prospect. He then removes his hooded jumper and pulls it over my head, followed by the cap. "Let's go for a walk." He grabs my hand and begins to lead me outside, but I pull back and he turns to face me.

"Out there?" I ask nervously.

"Come on, Six. It ain't like you haven't been out before. I know you and Cam took many secret trips out."

"But that's before I knew everything I know now," I argue. He laughs, shaking his head before tugging me harder to follow him.

"You're with me, you're safe."

The streets are busy. Cam and I only really ever went out late in the evening. It always amazed me that people were still out and about at those times, and I thought it was busy then, but nothing compares to now. The hustle and bustle is too much, and I cling to Dice like my life depends on it. He weaves us in and out of the human traffic like an expert and then we stop next to a street food cart, where he orders us a burger each and some drinks. Then, he leads me over the road to a park. There are people lounging about on the grass, enjoying the evening sun, and it's much quieter here, so I begin to relax. We find a space and sit, then Dice hands me my burger and we eat in silence. I enjoy people watching, so I don't mind.

Once Dice has eaten, he screws up his wrapper and lies back on the grass. "Is therapy helping?"

I think over his question. "Yes," I reply, "but she isn't telling me things I didn't already know."

"Really, like what?"

"I've been in denial for years. The things that were happening around me were obvious, and I turned a blind eye."

"I remember you as that defiant little troublemaker," he says, smiling. "You'd take the biggest beatings from your father, but you'd still go behind his back and do shit you shouldn't."

"Why didn't you ever go to the police?" I ask, wrapping up the remainder of my burger.

"Because I was like you, in denial. And when I realised what the hell had been going on and how wrong it was, I'd found the club and was beginning to rebuild my life. I didn't want anything to do with The Circle. But as I got older, I still couldn't get you from my mind, so I began looking for you again."

"I cried when you left," I admit, picking at the grass. "My father was so angry, he locked me away from everyone for such a long time. He only let me out when I became compliant. By then, Cam was training to be a man of god, which was lucky because my father let me hang around him, thinking he'd teach me all about our god and what was expected of me."

"And did he?"

I laugh, shaking my head. "I think we both know Cam isn't a man of god. Well, not for The Circle. He did it to protect himself, just like I turned a blind eye to protect myself. We didn't know what else to do. We couldn't leave because we had nothing and nowhere to go. No access to money meant we were dependent on The Circle. We talked about going to the police once, right after you left, but we were scared they wouldn't believe us."

"Cam started to record things," he says. "He was trying to build evidence so he could take you to the police and get you out. But I found you first."

I cross my legs and look down at his sun-kissed face. "Did you threaten to chop off his fingers?"

He smirks. "I needed to get access to you."

"So, you threatened him?"

Dice laughs. "It sounds much worse than it actually was." We fall silent again, both lost in thought. Eventually, Dice sits up. "What were you and Rylee discussing?"

"She was explaining things to do with money, like how bills work. She offered to let me help out in the women's centre as a way to earn for myself. She thinks I should help in the coffee shop, so I can get used to handling money."

"That's a good idea," he agrees.

"And then I'll be ready to step out into the big wide world," I say, lowering my eyes. The thought of leaving the club, even with Cam, makes me sick to my stomach. I'm safe at the club and even safer with Dice.

"Sounds like she's got everything in hand," he says, laying back down.

My heart twists. Half of me hoped he'd tell me I didn't need to leave the club. "Yeah. And Meli and Rosey want me to go on a night out, but I'm not so sure about that one." I give a nervous laugh.

"Maybe you'll enjoy it. You've missed out on so much . . . drinking, dating . . ." He trails off, and I shrug.

"I guess."

"You have your freedom back, Six. You should celebrate it."

A few days pass and I hardly see Dice. Rosey made a comment about him rolling the dice and hitting the road, but I hate he didn't say goodbye. I don't have time to dwell on it because the women have made sure to keep me busy. First, Rylee got me in the women's centre and helping in the café. I love it there, and all the women are amazing and friendly. Rosey set me up a mobile phone. Though I have no idea how to work it, it's nice to know help is just a button away . . . once I figure out which button that is. Hadley gave me more books that were less smutty than what Rosey gave me. *Pride and Prejudice* is my new favourite and I can't put it down.

Tonight, they're helping me dress up nice so we can have drinks in the club's bar. I don't feel ready to go out of the club, and Mav agreed it was too risky. I've never drank alcohol, apart from the night with Cam when I met Dice, so this will be another new experience.

Meli holds out a short dress, and I shake my head. "It doesn't have straps," I point out.

"I know, it's not supposed to."

"You'll see my bra straps."

"You don't wear a bra with it." She rolls her eyes, shoving me into the bathroom with the dress. I stare at myself in the mirror, but I don't recognise the woman staring back. Meli cut my hair today, it's always been long, right down to my waist, but now, it hangs to the middle of my back. She gave it layers, something I'd never heard of before, but I like it. The front shapes my face well, and somehow, I look my age instead of like a teenager. But the old me is whispering words my father used to say, that out here in the big world, evil washes away your pureness and you become like the devil, dressing like the rest of them to get a man's attention. *Is that what I'm doing?* Dice isn't even here, and I can't stand the thought of other men looking at me. I shake my head, trying to push the doubts away. This is my new life.

I get into the dress and run my hands down the sides. I look . . . sexy. The door opens and Meli stops in her tracks, her eyes wide as she takes me in. "Jeeeeez," she whispers. "You look amazing."

I smile shyly, but I feel fantastic. "Thanks."

She takes me by the shoulders and pushes me back into my room, sitting me on the chair. "Now, makeup."

"Oh, I've never worn it," I say, suddenly nervous. "Maybe that's a step too far."

"Lady, I have so much to teach you. Makeup enhances your beauty. It makes you feel good, and that's what's important."

The music is pumping as we head downstairs and through the main room. The other women are already in the bar, and as I enter, they smile. "You look amazing," says Rylee, kissing me on the cheek. "Dice would die if he saw you like this."

"That can be arranged," says Rosey, snapping a picture. I blink, the flash hurting my eyes.

"You have his number?" I ask, hating the fact I don't, even though I wouldn't know how to contact him anyway.

She glances up from her phone, then at the others. "Yeah, I can give it to you."

"No, it's fine. I mean, he doesn't know I have a phone, so it would be weird if I—"

"He knows," Rosey announces, tapping away on her phone. "I sent him your number."

I bite my lower lip, realising he could have contacted me but he's chosen not to. Rylee senses my upset and smiles brightly. "Anyway, shall we drink?" She leads me to the bar. "Let's start with something nice, like white wine," she tells Copper, who's behind the bar, and he gets us a bottle and some glasses. I take my glass from Rylee and sip it. It's not too bad, sweet and cold, so I nod and she smiles in relief. "Great, but take it easy. This stuff can be lethal."

I sit amongst the women and listen to the way they chat so easily around one another. The women in The Circle didn't get together. We stuck to our own households, and the only time we'd really see others was on market days, where we'd take our home-grown produce and share it around the families. Even then, we'd share pleasantries but nothing more.

Gracie leans into me. "It must feel strange for you," she says.

"I've never really done this," I tell her. "And I've never drank alcohol."

"Did you have many friends?"

I shake my head. "Only Cam."

"He's amazing. The kids here have really taken to him. We'll be sorry when he leaves, when you both leave. But it's exciting, you have a whole life to lead now." I nod in agreement, but the ache in my heart doesn't lift. "You don't seem happy about it."

"I am happy," I say, trying to sound convincing, "but a bit apprehensive about leaving here."

"You'll always be a welcome visitor."

We're interrupted when some of the men come in, rowdy and loud. Copper begins serving them, and some of the women go off to greet their men. Dice isn't amongst them, and I realise how much I'm missing him. Tatts sits in a vacant seat beside me. "You look sad," he points out.

"No, just taking it all in." I finish my second glass of wine, and he pours me another.

"You look gorgeous, by the way."

I blush. "Thank you." I feel slightly dizzy, but I'm so relaxed, it feels nice.

"When you eventually get out there to the bars, you'll be beating men off."

"You think?"

"I know. In fact, I might have to follow you around and scare them away."

I laugh. "How will I find a man if you scare them all away?"

"You won't. Then you'll have to settle for me." He grins, and I blush deeper, biting my lower lip to hide my smile. He groans and his thumb presses against my chin, pulling my lip free. "Dice hasn't claimed you?" he asks.

I shake my head, not really understanding the question. "I don't think so."

"Remember when you asked me to help you out?" I nod. "If you still need help with that, just say the word."

"I got a word for yah. *Snake* . . . that's a good one. Or dick . . . that's another." We both look up into the angry face of Dice. "Now, you got less than five seconds to get the fuck away from her before I start beating on a brother."

Tatts grins, standing. "Relax. You ain't laid claim, so what's a brother to do when she's sitting there all coy, biting that lip?"

"Have some damn respect," Dice yells. "She ain't like other women, and you know it."

"You're back," I murmur, surprised to see him.

"You're almost naked," he grits out, and I look down at my dress. "And makeup . . . that your thing now?"

"I . . . Meli just . . ." I rub a hand over my cheek, feeling the burn of embarrassment. He looks disgusted.

"Meli should have kept her dresses and makeup to herself," he snaps. He brings the dice from his pocket and shakes them in his hand. He blows on them before rolling them out on the table. We both watch as they roll to a stop. "Look at that," he mutters, grabbing me by the hand. "Double six."

DICE

I know she's struggling to keep up with me in the heels she's wearing, but I didn't expect to roll in my favour, and I have to hurry the fuck up before I change my mind. I fling open my bedroom door, pulling her inside and slamming it closed. "You look fucking good," I say. I'm too pumped after finding our lead on The Circle was a dead end, so I know the last place I should be is here, alone, with her. But the dice decided, and so far, they haven't steered me wrong.

"I thought you didn't like it," she says, tugging uncomfortably at the hem of the skirt.

I take her hand and spin her so I can see the back. It's just below her arse, so I pull it up, taking in her peachy backside in the black thong she once turned her nose up at. "What the fuck is this?" I ask, hooking my finger in the piece of material and giving it a gentle tug.

"Meli said it's so no one can see the VPL. I don't know what that means, but I didn't argue, she was so kind helping me."

I turn her to face me. "I rolled a double six," I tell her, sitting on the bed.

"Is that a good thing?" she asks, sounding unsure.

I shrug, because I'm still not certain myself, but for one night, I feel like being fucking selfish, so I pull her closer until she's in front of me. "I missed you," I tell her. "And I missed this." I touch her pussy under the dress, and she inhales sharply. I pull her onto me, so her legs are either side of mine, and her dress automatically rolls up. I lie back, tapping her arse until she begins to climb up my body. "We're gonna do a thing," I tell her, gripping the thong between my hands and ripping it apart. She gasps. "And this was in my way." I drop the thong onto the bed beside us, then I push my hands under her arse and lift her. She yelps as her knees land either side of my head, and I pull her down onto my waiting mouth.

"Malachi," she cries, slamming her hands against the wall for balance. She tastes fucking good, and when she begins to grind against my mouth, any sane thoughts I had completely vanish. I roll her over until she's laying on the bed. Kneeling between her legs, I look down at her rolled-up dress and her dishevelled hair, and she's never looked more beautiful. I wipe my thumb over her lipstick. "You don't need this," I whisper. "You're fucking gorgeous, Rae."

"Are you going to have sex with me?" she whispers, and I nod. She bites her lower lip and half smiles.

Taking a condom from my wallet, I unfasten my jeans as Six watches. I grip my shaft, pumping it until it's solid, and then I rip the packet open and slide the condom over my length. She's wet, so I rub the head of my cock between her folds. She pants, closing her eyes. "Relax," I whisper, slowly pushing against her entrance. I can feel her tensing, so I lower my mouth to hers, softly kissing as I ease into her. It's enough to distract her until I'm almost fully inside. She flinches, gripping my shoulders. "Nearly there," I reassure her, looking down between us and watching as I stretch her open. Once I'm in as far as I can get without hurting her more, I still, kissing her again. "You're doing great," I tell her.

"It hurts," she pants.

I nod, kissing her nose. "It gets better, I promise." I withdraw slowly, watching every wince on her pretty face. "The worst part is over now."

She breathes a sigh of relief, and I feel her relax a little. "Does it hurt you?"

I smile at her cuteness. "No, Six. To me, it's the best feeling in the world." I bend her leg at the knee and begin to move again. "Is this okay?"

She nods. "It feels . . . fuller."

"I'm gonna try and go slow, Six, but fuck, you're killing me."

I rub my thumb over her clit to distract myself from wanting to fuck her senseless. Slow and careful isn't my style, but with Rae, it's different. I want her to feel special and cared for. I want her to enjoy it as much as she can for her first time. She begins to writhe beneath me, her cheeks flush, and she's breathing hard. Grabbing onto my shoulders, she digs her nails into the skin. "It's too much," she whispers, looking panicked.

"It's perfect," I assure her, watching her lose control as her orgasm takes over her body. Her pussy grips my cock tight, and I release into the condom, groaning into her neck. *She's perfect.*

We fall silent, the only sound in the room is our heavy breathing.

"Was it okay?" she asks. "Did I do it right?"

I push myself up so I'm looking down on her. My cock is still semi-hard, and I try and think clean thoughts to make it go down. "You did everything right," I tell her. "It was perfect. And I promise, it gets better."

I withdraw and notice the blood coating her inner thighs. "Oh my god," she cries. "Did I hurt you?"

I can't help the laugh that escapes me. "No, Six. It happens the first time you have sex. No one is hurt."

I take her hand and lead her to the bathroom, where I turn on the shower. Once it's warm, I direct her into it while I wrap the condom and throw it in the bin. Then, I join her under the warm spray. Taking the sponge, I wash her down, paying close attention between her legs. She then takes the sponge and runs it over my chest. "Thank you," she whispers.

I kiss her gently. "You gave me the most precious gift, Six. You don't need to thank me."

CHAPTER THIRTEEN

ASTRAEA

I wake with Dice wrapped around me. His leg is thrown over my own and his arm is like a dead weight around my stomach. He was right—sex gets better after the second and third time.

I twist, carefully sliding from his grasp and slipping out of bed. Pulling on his shirt, I head downstairs for a drink, but I slow by Mav's office. The lights are on and the door is slightly open. I can hear Mav's voice, but the reason I stop is because I hear Rylee mention my name. "I just don't think it's safe for Rae to be cast out like this," she says, sounding angry.

"I know, and I get what you're saying, but I trust Dice and his decision."

"Mav, he makes decisions by rolling a fucking set of dice. This is her life we're talking about. You have no idea where The Circle are, and he just wants to stick her in some run-down bedsit with Cam. Out of sight, out of mind."

I feel my heart speed up. "That's not how it is, and you know it. He cares about her. If he didn't, he wouldn't be helping her."

"But not enough to claim her and keep her here at the club where she'll be safe."

"It's a lot to ask of him. His life went from carefree to serious very quickly. Dice has never been good at settling down, and he hasn't made Rae any promises. He's done so much for her already, it's time for her to make it alone. It's what he wants, and he's my priority, Ry. You know the club comes first."

"So, you agree she needs to move out of the club ASAP?"

"If that's what Dice wants, then yeah."

I turn back around to the stairs and creep up, only this time, I go to my own room, locking the door and falling onto my bed while clutching my aching heart. I thought he liked me, yet all this time he's been trying to get rid of me. My heart hurts worse than it ever has. The Circle may have been fucked-up, but at least I never felt this sort of pain. And worst of all, I gave him the one thing he wanted, so he's got no reason to keep me around for a second longer.

"Six, open the door!" I stir, stretching out and glancing at the clock beside my bed. It's seven a.m. and Dice bangs on the door louder. "Six, are you okay?"

I sigh, throwing the sheets back and getting up to open the door. He stares at me, looking me up and down like he's checking I'm in one piece. "I woke and you were gone. Are you okay?" He looks genuinely concerned, but he's become so good at acting lately, I don't know if he's faking it.

"I'm fine. I just wanted to sleep in here," I say, forcing a smile.

He narrows his eyes. "You're upset."

"No, not at all," I lie.

He steps closer, wrapping his arms around my waist and holding me against him. I try to relax, but he doesn't fall for it. "Okay, there's definitely hostility here. What did I do?"

"Honestly, you're paranoid. I have to shower. I'm helping with the breakfast today, and then I'm going to the women's centre with Rylee."

He almost pouts with disappointment. "I thought we could spend the day together. Maybe get out of here?"

"I can't let the girls down."

"They'll understand. I'll explain."

I step away, and his arms fall to his sides. "You've been away for days, and I've got a good routine going, so you can't just come back and expect me to drop everything."

His smile fades, and I can tell he wants to push the questioning further, but instead, he shrugs. "Yeah, you're right. Sorry. You go and help Rylee. I'll find something to keep me busy."

"Okay."

"And you're sure you're okay?" I nod, grabbing the door and waiting for him to leave. He eyes me suspiciously as he passes. "We'll talk later?" I nod again.

I find Cam in his room. "Did anyone mention us moving out?" I ask.

"Rylee talked about us sharing a place together when we're ready to leave."

"I overheard them talking last night, Rylee and Mav. She said Dice asked her to find us somewhere as soon as possible. He wants us gone."

Cam sits up. "Are you sure?"

"Yeah. The thing is, Cam, I like him," I admit. "Really like him. And to know he doesn't feel the same, it makes everything inside me hurt."

"Rae, you don't know that. Speak to him. He went to so much trouble to find you, and I don't believe for one second he doesn't love you."

"I heard them. He doesn't want me here, and I don't want to be a burden. I'm embarrassed enough."

"What does that mean?" He looks worried. "Don't do anything stupid, Rae, not until you've spoken to him."

"I can't speak to him. He'll never admit it. I just want to make it easier on us both. I think we should leave."

He looks alarmed. "What? We have no idea how to live alone. We'll never be able to do it."

"People do it all the time. Kids run away from home and live on the streets and survive. We'll work it out. We've always looked after each other."

"I guess I could call Josephine and find out where she is. She could help."

"She left? When?"

"A couple of days ago. I tried calling, but she didn't answer. I'll try again and leave a message asking if she can help us."

"Okay, I've got to help Rylee now. I think you should come and meet me at the centre in about an hour. I can slip out, and she won't realise we've gone until after closing."

"Why are we sneaking out if he wants you to leave anyway? Just tell them."

I shake my head. "I can't look him in the face and tell him I'm leaving without either breaking down or having a full-blown panic attack. It's easier on us both like this."

DICE

We're in church and the brothers are talking about our failed attempts at tracking The Circle. I'm tuned out because all I can think about is Six and why she was acting so weird earlier today. Everything was perfect last night. By the third time, she was climbing on me and asking me to show her how I liked it. When I woke to find her gone, a panic took hold of me, and now, I can't shake the feeling of dread in my stomach. I knew this would happen. It was the reason I told myself to stay away from her, but now, I've sealed both our fates because I'm not giving her up. I can't.

"Are you even listening?" snaps Grim, bringing me from my thoughts.

"Huh?"

"Is it possible they've gone for good? We've tracked the flights for Saturday and that rich arsehole isn't on any. He hasn't returned to the U.K. Maybe they've given up on Rae and have crawled back into a hole?"

I shake my head. "I don't know, but I doubt it. Besides, there are other girls suffering, and we can't just forget about them."

"But we can relax if Rae isn't in any immediate danger. You wanted her shipped out of here, right? That can happen if The Circle has left town," says Mav.

"About that," I mutter. "Tell Rylee to hold off finding them a place. Things have changed."

Mav grins. "Good to know, brother. Did you have any luck finding your fake mute?"

I shake my head. I've been trying to contact Talina for days, but she's not answering my calls. "I'm gonna take a ride out to her mum's. I'm worried The Circle took her with them."

"I tried to help her, brother. Her and her mum," says Mav. "Her mum isn't ready for help, and Talina wouldn't leave her."

"I know, Pres, she's stubborn. I'll see if I can talk her round."

I come to a stop outside the run-down house where I always drop Talina off. The garden is overgrown, and the front door is worn with chipped brown paint. The glass panel in it is broken, and when I find the door locked, I reach in through the window to release the safety latch. My boots crunch on broken glass in the hallway. "Talina," I shout. "It's Dice." There's no response, so I step farther inside. The kitchen is a mess, with dirty dishes stacked on every surface and discarded rubbish scattered amongst them. I spot a mouse running across the floor and shake my head in disgust. Poor Talina.

The living room is in much the same disorganised, dirty state. "Tali," I try again, but there's still nothing.

Heading upstairs, I come to the first door and tap gently before entering. I find Talina's mum passed out naked on a bed, a used needle beside her and a tourniquet still wrapped around her arm. I move closer, pressing my fingers to her neck to check she's still alive. There's a pulse, so I release the rubber band and she stirs, rolling over to her side and groaning.

I go to the next room, easing the door open to find it clean and tidy. Talina is asleep on the bed, and I breathe a sigh of relief. As I move closer, I see she's taken a beating. Her eyes have faded bruises and her mouth has a tinge of yellow and blue around it. "Tali," I whisper, gently touching her shoulder. Her eyes shoot open, and she inhales sharply. I jump back. "It's okay. It's just me," I whisper. She's sits, her breathing coming out in rapid bursts. "Do you know how worried I've been?" I ask. "I've tried calling you a hundred times." She stares at me blankly, and her behaviour is odd. "Are you high?" I snap, grabbing her chin so I can check her pupils. She winces and tears fill her eyes. "Talina, what's going on?"

She slowly opens her mouth, and my blood runs cold. "They cut out your tongue?" I mutter. She closes her mouth and turns her head to release it from my grip. Then she lies back on the bed and pulls the sheet over her. I stare at her for a few silent minutes. "You can't stay here," I mutter. "Talina, you can't stay here. You're coming back to the club with me. I'm gonna get you help." She shakes her head, and I crouch beside the bed so we're at eye level. "Please. Please. I'll bring your mum too, but you can't stay in this hellhole. I can get you help." Tears fill her eyes. "I'm gonna make them pay, Tali, I swear to fucking God."

I put a call into Mav to send a car while Talina packs a bag for her and her mum. I wait outside, pacing with anger. The urge to get revenge is stronger than ever . . . for Mum, for Astraea, and now for Talina.

ASTRAEA

I wipe the sides down where I've spent the morning making coffee for the endless women Rylee has welcomed into the centre today. She's amazing with them, and no problem seems too big or too small. Her mobile shrills from her pocket and she answers it, moving slightly away. The frown on her face tells me it's not a happy call, and when she disconnects a minute later, she looks upset. "We have to close," she says. "Dice is bringing in a woman who needs help. I'm meeting them at the club."

I look around at the few women remaining. "I could close up," I tell her. "After they've finished their coffee."

"No, it's fine, they'll understand," she says, beginning to pull a shutter down at the window.

"Rylee, honestly, I can do it. I've watched you do it. I'll lock up and come straight back to the club. It's literally up the street, what can go wrong?" She bites on her lip, thinking it over. "Come on, I thought you were helping me become more independent?"

"If you're sure?"

"One hundred percent. Go, Dice needs you."

She kisses me on the cheek. "Okay. Here's the spare keys to lock up. Just post them back through the door. Thanks, Rae. See you soon."

It's another ten minutes before the final two women hand me their cups and thank me before leaving. Cam's been outside waiting, so I rush to lock up and post the keys back through the door. "Finally," he mutters, handing me a rucksack with my clothes. "That was the longest ten minutes of my life."

"Did anyone question you leaving?"

He shakes his head. "No. Dice brought two women back and it was all hands on deck to sort a room and medical attention. I snuck out in the midst of it all, and," he pulls out an envelope, "I got us some cash."

My eyes widen. "You stole from the club?"

"I borrowed. Mav asked me to stick it on his desk when he was rushing out earlier. I left a note saying I'll repay every penny."

"You left a note?" I almost screech.

"I couldn't just take it, Rae."

"But you left a note, which means he's gonna realise we've gone, and soon."

"He's too busy right now. Besides, if they wanted rid of us, why would they come looking?"

A car slows to a stop and Josephine sticks her head out. "Let's go," she says, smiling.

We throw our bags in, and I get in the back. "Thanks for this, Josephine," I say.

"Not a problem. Happy to help."

I smile, staring out the window as she pulls away. It crosses my mind to ask how she learned to drive, but I don't want to upset her over the whole divide thing at The Circle. It's possible they let her learn like they'd let Cameron.

We drive for at least an hour, and I find myself falling asleep throughout the journey, the gentle rocking making me sleepy. When we stop, I sit up and look around. We're at the gates of a huge house.

I've never seen anything like it. "Wow," I murmur, "this is beautiful. Is it a hotel?"

"Sort of," says Josephine, waiting for the gates to slide open before driving us along the stone driveway.

"It's huge," says Cam. "How did you find it?"

"I have my contacts," she says, winking.

"Contacts?" he repeats. "But you don't know anyone outside The Circle."

"I didn't say they were outside of it," she says, shrugging.

My blood runs cold and my heart hammers in my chest. Cam looks back at me, and I see the same panic in his eyes. "You went back?" he whispers.

"I never left," she says, laughing. "They knew where you were all along. They just couldn't get to you, so they set it up knowing your stupid biker boyfriend would take me back to their club and I could get some intel."

"Then why didn't they come, if they knew where we were?" I ask, hardly believing this is happening.

"I'll give biker boyfriend that, his security around that place is top notch. We had to wait for you to step outside, and even then, you were covered. He always had someone watching you from a distance. He really loves you, it's pathetic. In the end, it worked out perfectly because you came to me."

"You set us up?" Cam asks in disbelief.

"Not you, just her," she says, smiling like a maniac.

"Why?" I whisper.

"Why?" she repeats, mimicking me. "Because I'm sick of hearing how you're so damn perfect. We're similar in so many ways, yet we live completely different lives, so when you left, he finally noticed me. He saw in me what you were lacking, and I'm not going to let him down. You made it so easy. You just walked out of your safe zone, and I couldn't have planned it better." She laughs again. "I'm sorry about this next part, Cam. I feel bad because we kind of had a connection, didn't we? You were so kind when they brought me back, thinking they'd rescued me. But God is so terribly upset with you right now, and it's at his request that I . . ." I watch in horror as she leans towards Cam, pressing a gun to his chest. "End you." She pulls the trigger and there's a quiet popping sound right before Cam slumps against her, his eyes wide with terror.

"Noooo!" I scream, shoving myself between the gap in the front seats. "Cam?" I shake him, but he's lifeless. His mouth is open and his eyes are still wide, but there's nothing but a gurgling sound coming from him. I grip his shirt in my fists and shake him harder. "Cam, wake up," I beg. "Please don't leave me."

I'm aware of the car door opening and a hand reaching in to grab me. I kick out, screaming as I grip

Cam's shirt tighter. The hand squeezes my inner thigh hard until I release his shirt and allow myself to be removed from the car.

I'm thrown over a shoulder and carried, kicking and screaming, into the house.

CHAPTER FOURTEEN

DICE

I'm sitting in church, waiting for Mav to start the meeting he called. I roll the set of dice over and over with no particular question in my mind, just a stomach filled with dread. I haven't managed to shake the feeling all day. I check my watch, seeing it's almost two in the afternoon. "What time did you say Six should be back?" I ask.

Mav shrugs. "I dunno. She told Rylee she'd watch the place while she helped here."

"And the prospects are watching her?"

He shakes his head. "No, I called everyone back when you called about Talina. But the centre is safe, brother. There's plenty of people around." I nod, and he bangs the gavel on the table to start the meeting. "Thanks for all rushing back to help out. Talina is doing good. The doc assessed her, but she'd already sought out medical assistance after the incident. Her mum is on a drip for dehydration and to reverse that shit she put in her arm. Talina wrote down what happened, confirming The Circle discovered she was lying about being a mute. They decided to make it a reality for her."

"That shit is messed up," mutters Tatts.

"We're gonna kill them," I say firmly, staring at the double six on the table. "We're not gonna stop until they're all dead."

"I hear you, brother," says Mav. "We all want the same thing. But that's not all Talina wrote down. They had someone here, on the inside... Josephine. That's how The Circle knew Talina wasn't a mute. Turns out, Jo is another daughter of Joseph."

"Astraea and Jo are sisters?" I ask, frowning.

"Half-sisters. Same dad, different mum. It seems Jo's just been waiting for her chance to shine in daddy's eyes. Dice, you need to break the news to Rae. We don't want Jo luring her away." I nod. "Actually, you could head over to the centre now. I have some cash that needs going in the safe there. Let me get it," he adds, heading out the room.

"What's the p-p-plan with Rae?" asks Scar. "You g-g-gonna make her your ol' lady?"

I nod. "Yeah, brother. If she'll have me."

He slaps me on the back. "Congrats."

Mav returns, staring down at a handwritten note. His eyes meet mine and the dread in my stomach deepens. "Brother, we have a situation."

ASTRAEA

I've been staring at the same four white walls, blankly, for an hour now. They took my phone, so I have no way of calling Dice. *Dice*, he's probably hating on me right about now. Cam left a note, so the club thinks I've left them willingly and won't come looking.

I stare out of the window. I'm at least three stories up and the window is locked. Plus, there are men walking the grounds with large dogs. Cam, *poor Cam*, I keep seeing his pale face as he slumped over in the car. I begin to sob again. He was trying to help me, always trying to help me, and I led him back here to his death. Sliding down the wall, I cry into my hands. I was an idiot to think I could make it.

I hear the key in the door and wipe my eyes, pushing to stand. My father walks in, followed by my brother and Josephine, who I note looks smug. I automatically lower my eyes and hang my arms by my side. "Here she finally is." My father circles me, and I feel his eyes burning into me with anger. "Looking like one of them. Smelling like one of them."

"With that defiant look in her eyes again," comments Ares. "We worked so hard to beat that out of you the first time."

"Get her out of these clothes," Father hisses.

Josephine grabs my shirt and tries to lift it over my head, but I shove her hard, and she falls back against Ares. "Don't fucking touch me, you murdering bitch," I hiss. The word surprises me too. I've never cursed before, but I'm so angry. Father slaps me hard. It takes a second for me to recover, and I close my eyes to stop the spinning sensation from taking me to the ground.

"You dare to use that language in front of me!" he roars. He grabs me by the throat and pins me to the wall. "Remove her clothes," he repeats, and Josephine unfastens my jeans and tugs them from my legs. Ares rips my T-shirt down the middle, dragging it from me. "Dressed like an alluring whore," Father adds, taking in my lace thong and bra. "The devil really has his hooks in you." I keep my eyes lowered, feeling ashamed and embarrassed. *How does he always have the power to make me feel this way?*

The door opens again, and this time, a man in a suit comes in. He assesses the scene before him, and when his eyes finally land on me, his nostrils flare. "I thought you said she'd be ready?"

"She will," my father replies, releasing my neck. I rub it, trying hard not to cry.

"She doesn't look ready," the man growls. "Leave us." I can see in my father's eyes, he's angry. I've never heard anyone boss him around before and it's obvious he's unhappy, but he chooses not to comment and leaves, taking Ares and Josephine with him.

The man waits until we're alone and then proceeds to circle me, just like my father did. "It's a good thing I like defiance," he murmurs. "I paid a lot of money for you, goddess. I've waited a long time."

"For what?" I ask, my voice quiet.

"To have a pure goddess. To marry you." He runs his finger along my collar bone, then leans closer and inhales.

"You wasted your money because I'm not marrying you," I whisper.

He grins. "Careful, we might end up in our first fight."

"I'm going to get out of here, and you'll never see me again."

He laughs loudly, throwing his head back. "Oh, goddess, it's going to be fun breaking you. I'll try to take my time, savour every second."

He pulls out a pocketknife, and I watch him warily as he circles me again. Gripping my thong, he slices through the lace material with ease, letting it fall to the floor. Then he unclips my bra and throws that to one side. "Better," he says, smiling. He runs the tip of the knife across my abdomen while he continues to circle. "I hope you fight."

"Count on it," I say, forcing my voice to sound more confident and certain, just like Rosey's.

DICE

I sit beside Talina's bed, watching her sleep. She's been out for four hours. The rest of the club have gone out to search for Six, but it's fruitless. We have no clue where The Circle is, or if they've gotten to Astraea and Cam. I've rang them too many times and they haven't picked up. Even my pleading text telling them I just want to know they're safe has been left unanswered.

I keep twisting the set of dice around my fingers, plotting all the things I'm going to do to the Lords when I finally get my hands on them, while watching my phone, waiting for Cam to tell me they're safe and happy. *Happy,* fuck, she has no idea what she's done to me walking out like that. I was ready to offer her the world, and she just left. Not even a goodbye. Just a fucking note from Cam saying he'd repay the money he took from Mav.

Talina stirs, her eyes flutter open, and she opens her mouth to speak, then lets out a frustrated cry, like she'd forgotten for a second that she has no tongue and reliving the reminder is too painful. I take her hand and give it a gentle squeeze. "There's every chance you'll talk again, Tali. I spoke to the doc, and he said with lots of speech therapy, it's possible. We'll get the best speech therapist in the world, I promise." She settles, leaving tears to stain the sides of her face as they roll from the corners of her eyes. "Your mum's awake. I can't lie and tell you she's happy about being here, but we're in negotiations," I say with a small laugh. "She'll come around to my way of thinking."

Talina squeezes my hand once, and I take that as a thank you. "Please, don't thank me. I feel like this is my fault. I should have forced you to come to the club a lot sooner. A part of me needed you to keep going back in The Circle to get information, which was for fuck all because Rae left me today," I say bitterly. More tears fall from her, and I gently squeeze her hand. "I'm terrified The Circle will get to her before I can find her. And if they do, and they realise she's not . . . she's not pure anymore, they're gonna hurt her." I sigh heavily. "I don't suppose you have any idea where The Circle went to?" She shakes her head sadly. "If they find her, this has all been for nothing."

It's late when the guys return empty-handed. I take off on my bike because I'm unable to handle church, where they're going to tell me there are no leads and I should respect her wishes and let her leave.

I stop next to the park where I ate burgers with Six. I get off my bike and go to the spot where I sat with her, lowering to the ground. Five minutes pass before Rosey strolls over. "No, Rosey. I can't deal with you right now."

"I was just walking by and saw you looking sad." She lowers to sit beside me.

"You find people, right? So, why can't you find The Circle or Six?"

"It's not that easy. I get my target's details, I know where they hang out, what hobbies they have, because whoever orders their hit supplies me with details," she replies. "I do my research using those as a starting point. They go about their business as usual because they're not suspecting someone wants them dead. Most of the time, I can walk right beside them or turn up to the bars they drink in because they don't suspect a woman is going to slit their throat."

I think over her words, then frown. "Hold on, you follow them, turn up where they are?"

She nods. "Most of the time. I like to research to know the best way to take them out. Yah know, like quiet times, who checks in on them, and so on."

"And you get the details from an agency?"

"Yep."

"Where they get random people requesting a hit man?"

"Or woman," she says defensively.

I narrow my eyes. "But you keep following me and turning up where I am," I say as I pull my gun, pointing it at her head. I slowly rise to my feet, and she keeps her eyes trained on me. "Is there a hit on me?" I ask.

She isn't fazed by my gun at her temple. She rolls her eyes. "You're so dramatic. It's a good thing this place is empty. And yes," she says with a sigh, "but it's not what you think."

"Bullshit. You were gonna kill me?"

"No, Mav wouldn't let me."

"Mav knows about this?" I almost screech, my eyes widening in surprise.

"He said to keep it quiet."

I back away, my gun still trained on her. "Stay the fuck away from me or I swear I'll kill you."

She shrugs. "Suit yourself. I was trying to help."

I get back to the club and head straight for Mav's office. "There's a hit on me?" I yell.

He sits back in his chair and throws down his pen. "Rosey told you?"

"You should have told me!"

"There was too much going on, brother. I didn't want to overload you."

"Is this them? The Circle?"

He nods. "We think so. Rosey's been trying to find out. An anonymous person put the call in to her agency. They requested a woman, hoping she'd seduce you. Rosey turned the hit down, but we can't be sure they didn't hire someone else."

"That's why Rosey's been up my arse."

"Hey, I've been keeping your arse safe," comes Rosey's voice as she saunters in behind me. "And actually, I was being nice the first few times I followed you. The hit came later."

"I don't need you to keep me safe. You should have told me. You know I hate secrets, Mav." I pace back and forth. "All this time, I thought we had the upper hand, and all along, they were one step ahead."

"It doesn't mean we can't get back on top, brother. We're working on it."

"We were never on top. She's gone, Pres. Astraea's gone. They've won."

"You don't even know if they've got her. She could be sleeping in a hotel somewhere safe, for all we know."

I shake my head. "Nah, I feel it. I've felt it all day. She walked out of here and into a trap."

"Pres, we've got an update," says Grim, barging into the office.

He glances at Rosey, who rolls her eyes. "We really need to have a conversation about girls being equal to boys," she says. "I can kill all of you with my eyes closed, but you won't let me in on club business. It's ridiculous." She leaves, and Grim closes the door.

"A body's been recovered. My cop on the inside sent me a picture. It's Cam."

"Fuck," mutters Mav. "You sure?"

"One hundred percent. And of course, the cops will never identify him cos he's not registered anywhere."

"Maybe it's time we let them deal with this," Mav suggests.

"No," I snap. "Prison is too good for those bastards. I want blood, Mav. I want to see the life fade from Joseph's eyes."

He rubs his forehead in frustration. "Roll the dice," he eventually says.

Grim groans. "Come on, Pres, don't encourage him."

I hold the dice, blowing and closing my eyes. "Even numbers, we do it my way. Odd, you can call the cops."

"Agreed," mutters Mav.

I roll the dice and they clatter across his desk, hitting the lamp. We all look at them, and I smile. Two and six. I snatch them up. "Let's draw up a map and mark all the areas near where Cam was found. They'll be in a secluded place, or one with high security measures."

CHAPTER FIFTEEN

ASTRAEA

It's been a couple of days since I was brought here, and I'm still in the same room as before. There's a single bed with a sheet, and I've been given a full-length night dress to wear. They bring me two meals a day, breakfast and dinner, and nothing between.

I've had no contact with any of my family, so when the door is unlocked and my mother comes in, I'm surprised. I smile, rushing to greet her, but she stands stiff as I wrap my arms around her. My smile fades and I pull back. "I missed you so much," I tell her. "I thought about you every day."

She stares at me blankly. I've never noticed the emptiness in her eyes. "I am so disappointed in you, Astraea," she says in a low voice. "So very disappointed."

"It wasn't my fault," I say. "I was taken."

"Because you were sneaking out with your friend. You corrupted a man of God and now he's dead. His death is on your hands."

I shake my head, shocked by her cruel words. "Josephine, she . . . she killed Cam."

"It was too late for him. You bewitched him with your alluring ways, encouraging him to sneak out with you and using him to help you leave us."

"I didn't choose to leave, I was taken," I repeat.

"I saw how you came back, dressed looking just like them. Did they force you to become just like them?" She gives a cold, empty laugh before adding, "You're evil."

"No, that's not how it was. They gave me those clothes, and I had to take them. I couldn't walk around naked. I tried to leave and come back at first, but they stopped me and then, over time . . . I . . . well, I began to question things."

"Josephine told us about Malachi. You let the devil get inside your head and you didn't put up a fight. You had chances to leave. They began to trust you, and yet you chose to stay. You were always so easily led, Astraea. Maybe there's a part of the devil in you."

"Mother, listen to yourself. This isn't real, any of it. They're killing girls for their own sick satisfaction. The Lords are the evil ones."

She rears back and slaps me hard. "I knew you were evil from the day you were born. Those little blue eyes taunted men, good men. Your father was bewitched, everyone was, but after that boy left, I believed you'd been redeemed, that God had accepted you. I can't hold my head up amongst the community because of what you've done. You will pay, Astraea. God will make you pay."

"God doesn't punish, not like that. Those men want sex, they want power and sex, and you can dress it any way you want to help you sleep at night, but we all know the truth. Those girls that disappear, they kill them for their own entertainment."

"They are chosen by God as a sacrifice. Do you know how many of them have been sacrificed to put right your wrongdoings?"

"Yet they didn't help. Don't you ever question why?"

She smirks. "Of course, they did. You're here, aren't you? God listened and returned you to where you belong."

I take a calming breath. Nothing I say will change her mind. I wonder if Dice felt these same frustrations when he first saw me again. "What will happen to me now?" I ask.

She smirks. "You're getting married, Astraea."

"To that man who came in here?"

"Robert? He's charming, isn't he?"

"He's a pig."

She slaps me again. "Be careful, Astraea, your defiance is not welcome here."

"And after the wedding? Will I live here, like you?" She shakes her head and begins to back out to the door. "Where will I go? With him?"

"Your husband will cure you of your evil, and our Lords will help. God chose you, Astraea, despite your little slip-up recently. There will be a huge ceremony, a celebration, and a sacrifice. It was always the plan. For the good of The Circle."

Panic fills me. "No, that's ridiculous. Why am I getting married if they're going to kill me? Why don't you question them? Why don't you ask who told them that God wants me? Who gave them the power to cleanse me of evil? Why aren't you asking them all of these questions?" I yell angrily.

"Our Lords are men of God. Their children are pure and belong to God. When it's time for them to return to him, it's a celebration, Astraea. You should be excited."

My thoughts are racing. "But I'm not pure," I blurt out. "I'm not innocent and pure anymore."

She eyes me suspiciously. "What do you mean?"

"I had sex. With Malachi."

Her expression turns thunderous. "You're lying. You wouldn't have had sex out of wedlock, Astraea. I know you."

"You know the pure me. But the devil me, you have no clue. I fucked him, over and over, and I loved it!" I spit angrily.

She stares wide-eyed for a few silent seconds and then she leaves without another word. I rush to the door, but she's already locking it as I hit against it. "Mother, let me out! He's coming for me. He'll save me, and you'll all pay," I scream through the wood. "You're all going to die."

DICE

It's been days. We've searched woodland, we've gone off-track and searched abandoned shacks, and we've even wandered around small villages on the outskirts, but there's no sign of Six or The Circle. Grim has his cops on the inside looking out for her, we sent a picture and told them she was one of the women coming to us for help to flee a violent marriage, but still, it's brought us nothing. I've called and called Cam's and Rae's phones, but both are turned off and neither device is coming up on our tracker. It's like they've all disappeared off the face of the earth.

Rosey joins me on the couch where I'm twisting the dice between my fingers. "I just found out something."

"Enlighten me."

"The hit on you has changed. We got a new offer."

I sit up straighter. "Does Mav know?"

She shakes her head. "Not yet. I thought I'd come to you first this time, since your hissy fit the other day over secrets. They want you. They've offered one hundred thousand for you to be taken to them, alive."

Hope fills me as I head straight for the office with Rosey behind me and relay the information to Maverick.

"No, absolutely not," he says.

"But this is how we find them," I say desperately.

"You said it yourself, they're one step ahead. I can't have any more bodies on my hands."

"You think she's dead?" I ask.

"I don't know, Dice. All I know is I'm not sending one of my men in there, and they're sure as hell not stupid enough to give out the address."

"They requested he goes in knocked-out," adds Rosey.

"Mav, they're not expecting Rosey to know me. They want me bad and they're putting money out there for me to be taken to them. This is the only lead we've had in ages."

"My answer is no."

"We have to vote on it," I say. "I want the brothers' vote."

Mav glares at me. "It's a suicide mission. You don't even know if they have Rae."

"There's no way she's out there, surviving alone without Cam. And it's no coincidence he's turned up dead. They have her, and I need to get to her."

Mav calls church and tells the brothers about the new developments. "I'm with Mav," agrees Grim. "It's a suicide mission. They want you dead."

"I didn't have to roll the dice," I say, "because I know this is the right thing to do. I can't stand not being near her. So, if I get there and they kill me, which I don't think they'll do, at least I'll die near her."

"With her," corrects Mav. "Cos that's what will happen. They're gonna make you watch her die and then kill you. You know that's a possibility. Why else would they want you alive?"

"Would you do it?" I ask. "For Rylee?" He doesn't reply, knowing I'm right. I sigh. "Look, I don't plan to go in there and let them just kill me. They pick on women for fuck's sake. I can take them on. But we can plant a tracker, right?" I look at Grim.

"I do have some new implant trackers to try."

"To try?" Mav repeats. "What if they're crap and don't work?"

"Then, like you said, we lose him, and I don't have to listen to the sound of those clanking little fucking cubes again. It's a win-win."

"Fuck, this is crazy," Mav mutters, rubbing his face.

"I reckon he's got a point," says Ghost. "He's got enough rage in him to take those fuckers down. Rosey doesn't have to knock him out to take him in. He can act until he's inside, they'll never know."

"I just don't like how they've been so ahead of us on everything," Mav admits. "If they have Astraea, they've got what they want, so why are they hanging around for you?"

"Because they know I'll keep coming for her and for them. I won't give up."

"We're out o-of time," says Scar. "It's our l-last hope of finding R-rae. We g-gotta trust D-dice can do it."

Mav shrugs helplessly. "Looks like I'm out-voted on this. But we go in with a good plan and a backup. I don't want a shitshow which ends with us burying one of our own. The only people allowed to die are those crazy cult fuckers."

ASTRAEA

Water is thrown over me and I wake with a start, coughing and spluttering, and I realise quickly that I'm being stripped naked again. Ares is smirking down at me with my father standing behind him. "Is it right?" he asks, his voice cold. "You're no longer pure?" I opt to keep my mouth closed because fear is gripping my chest like a vice. "Very well, we'll find out for ourselves."

I scoot back on the bed, trying to get away, but Ares snatches my ankle and drags me towards him. The door opens and a man in a white coat enters. I've never seen him before, but I know The Circle has their own doctors. Ares takes my arms and holds them above my head. I begin thrashing around, kicking out, and the doctor looks at my father and shrugs helplessly, unsure of what to do with me when I'm making it so difficult for him. My father holds up a long device and presses it against my side. A blue light flashes and pain shoots across my stomach. I scream, and Ares covers my mouth with his hand. "Lie still and open your legs, or I'll do it again," Father warns.

I stare up at the ceiling, tears leaking from the corners of my eyes. The doctor positions my legs by pushing my feet together and pulling my knees apart. I shut down as he pushes something cold and hard inside me. After a minute, he removes the object. "She's not a virgin," he confirms.

Father's eyes are full of rage, and the second the doctor leaves, he presses the rod to my thigh, then my stomach, and then my breast, holding it longer each time. I writhe in pain, screaming until my throat is sore. "You whore," he roars. "Do you know what this means?"

"That you can't use me to sacrifice because God won't want me," I scream, trying hard to fight Ares off.

"No, Astraea, it means I'm going to make the final few days of your life absolute hell."

"Oh, trust me, I'm already there," I scream.

Ares grips my throat, squeezing tightly until black spots blur my vision. The last thing I see is his smirk as my eyes close.

CHAPTER SIXTEEN

DICE

Rosey took the job, and now, we're playing it safe and acting how Rosey would normally act if she were to stalk her prey. If she contacts them too soon, they'll be suspicious, but if she waits too long, Six could be in more danger. So, I must go about business like I'm not raging inside and wanting to rip the world apart to find her. That's why I find myself working a shift at Dice's. I've neglected the place since Six came back into my life.

After closing, I sit in the office and check over the books. Stacy has done a great job of running the place, and I make a note to give her a pay rise. Once I get Six home again, it'll take us time to settle down and I probably won't be around so much.

"I'm getting pretty tired waiting around for you, can we go home now?" asks Rosey, flopping down on a chair opposite me.

"Aren't you supposed to stay out of my sight or something?"

"I'm bored." She sighs, tapping impatiently on the desk. "It's no fun when you know I'm watching you."

"You told me to go about my business."

"They didn't give much information on you. I asked my usual questions, and all they knew was you were in an MC. They're not as clued up as we thought. Do you think she's okay?"

I shrug. I've tried not to think about what Six will be going through because I know it'll be bad. "I hope so."

"Are you worried they'll turn her back into one of them?"

"No. She knew all along the kind of people they are, but she was in survival mode."

"I think we should move tomorrow."

"Ready when you are, Rosey. The sooner, the better." I instantly relax because it's what I've been waiting for.

"I'll call the contact number tomorrow and ask where the drop-off is. Let's hope it's their doorstep, so we both get to kill them."

ASTRAEA

Every muscle in my body is screaming in pain. I curl into a tight ball, but it's no use and doesn't do anything to stop the pain of the electricity they keep putting through my body. I've been kicked, punched, and spat at. I've been called every name under the sun, but I force myself to smile through it, because I know, without a doubt, that Dice is coming for me. My smile infuriates them more. They keep telling me it's the devil inside of me, and maybe they're right. Maybe it's always been there, and I hid it to live a simple life, but now I've had a taste of the outside world, I want it all the more.

I'm hauled to my feet. "Shower her. I'm going to begin the ceremony. I'll send Josephine to get her," Father snaps, shoving me towards Ares.

I'm exhausted and unsteady on my feet as he drags me from the bedroom and into a bathroom. He turns the water on cold and pushes me to stand underneath the spray. I inhale sharply, and he grins. I catch a glimpse of my beaten and bruised body in the mirror and wince. I look a mess. Reaching for a bar of soap, I begin to wash, all under the watchful eye of my brother. It makes my skin crawl. The door opens and Josephine pops her head in. A silent communication passes between the pair before Ares turns to me. "Hurry, you should be out when I return." Then he steps out, keeping hold of the door to let me know he's right outside.

I leave the shower running but step out, carefully opening a drawer. There's nothing inside, and I clench my teeth in frustration. Opening the medicine cabinet, I almost jump for joy when I spot a metal nail file. I grab a towel, turn off the shower, and wrap myself up, tucking the nail file under my arm. "I'm done," I say.

We get back into my room, and Ares leaves me alone to dress in a clean white cotton dress. I hide the nail file under the thin mattress and dress quickly. Josephine returns minutes later, holding the electric rod. "No funny business," she warns.

I'm led into a large sauna. Men in cloaks, their hoods up, line the outer walls. I can't see faces, but I'm certain they'll be peeking as Josephine removes my dress. She points to the pool of water, and I get in, lowering until my body is submerged. I would often have to bathe with the Lords. Other girls would be present too, helping to wash them. I never saw the same girls twice, and now I know much more, I'm certain those girls were killed.

The Lords file into the room, losing their cloaks and lowering into the pool with me. They seat themselves around the edge until I am surrounded. My father glares at me, leaning his arms back over the edge and giving me a smug smile. "Our goddess is back with us. Our cleansing can begin."

DICE

The small metal chip is inserted into my inner thigh. Ghost had to get way too close to my junk so the small incision was hidden well, and now, we're both avoiding eye contact as Grim preps me on how the thing works. He shows me a screen on his phone, and there's a green flashing circle on a map of the area. "That's you," he tells me, like I'm stupid. "So, once we get a location, we'll come rescue your crazy arse."

"If we're down to the wire," I say, but Mav begins to protest, telling me the plan is fool proof. I hold up my hand, and he stops talking. "I don't want you to rescue me. You get to Six and the other girls. You come for me last."

"We're coming for you all," Grim reassures me. "And we'll get you all out alive."

Rosey steps forward. "They want you in naked," she tells me, and the guys snigger.

"Is that true or are you making that up so you can check me out?" I ask, shrugging out of my kutte and handing it to Mav to look after.

"I've been watching you, I've seen you naked," she says, shrugging.

I kick off my boots. "One question, aren't they gonna get suspicious? Won't they question how you got me naked?"

She rolls her eyes. "Because I'm such a small, defenceless girl?" she asks, her voice dripping with sarcasm. "If I wanted you butt naked, I could do that. But as it happens, I have these," she says, pointing to her breasts, "and they're usually enough to get any red-blooded male naked."

When I'm fully naked, I hold out my wrists. "Have you checked to make sure we ain't being watched?" I ask Grim.

"No one around here for miles," he confirms, checking the drone screen that Scar is currently operating.

Rosey wraps thick rope around my wrists and ties it with expertise. I try to break it with no success, and she grins, satisfied she's impressed me. "I don't even want to know how you learned your rope tying skills," mutters Mav, shaking his head.

Rosey winks playfully. "Are you ready?" she asks, and I nod. I bend lower so she can tie a gag around my mouth. "Showtime."

ASTRAEA

I lie on my bed, shivering from the cold. My hair is wet, but my body has now dried from the air. Every time I close my eyes, I picture those men releasing into the water of the pool. I can smell them on me, and I can still hear their chants about cleansing me and keeping the devil from me. I shudder. How did I ever think this was normal?

I hear the sound of tyres on the stone driveway down below. I haven't heard anyone arriving or leaving, so I get up and stare down as a car stops by the front door. A man in a hooded cloak rushes down the steps to greet whoever it is, pulling open the car door. "He's completely out," I hear a man say. "You need a wheelchair to move him."

I watch as a wheelchair is wheeled to the back passenger side. More men in cloaks join them, and after some pulling and pushing, someone is lifted out of the backseat by their arms and lowered into the chair. His body slumps to one side, and as the chair is turned towards the house, the moonlight catches his face and I gasp. *Dice.* They have Dice. I grip the bars blocking my window, stopping myself from screaming his name. How did this happen? Was he looking for me? Did I lead him here? I fall back onto the mattress just as the bedroom door opens and Ares saunters in. "You've seen our visitor then?" He smirks.

"Why is he here?" I snap.

"He's a guest to your wedding, sister. Aren't you pleased to see him?"

He moves closer, and I back away. "Get out."

He trails his finger over my ankle. "I've been thinking," he mutters, stopping with his hand on my knee. "Seeing as you're no longer pure, no one would know if I was to—"

"I'd tell them," I hiss, shoving his hand from me.

He grabs my ankle, yanking me hard until I'm flat on my back. I twist away, and he climbs over me, pinning me face down onto the mattress. "We're not blood related," he whispers in my ear. "No one knows who belongs to who. You might not even be their real daughter." His hand holds me by the back of the neck while his other travels down my side. I thrash around as I reach for the nail file, keeping his attention on restraining me. When I get a good grip, I relax, and he eases up on holding me so tight.

"Okay," I pant. "You're hurting me. Let me breathe," I add.

He lifts slightly, and I turn onto my back. His eyes are immediately drawn to my breasts, and he grins. "I had the doc run some extra tests," he tells me, dragging his finger down the centre of my chest, "because your breasts have changed since I last saw you." I frown, wondering how long he's been paying such close attention to my body. "I took your piss from the bucket," he adds, nodding to my makeshift toilet in the corner of the room. "Seems you and the devil created evil together." He prods my stomach and shudders. "Another evil life."

"What?" I whisper, confused.

He grabs my breasts, squeezing hard, and I cry out. "You're pregnant, you stupid slut. So, I have a deal. I get to fuck the goddess and I'll keep your secret from the Lords."

"I'm going to die anyway, so I don't care if they know," I hiss, trying to push him from me.

"Do you know what they'll do if they find out about this?" he asks, leering down at me with evil delight in his eyes. "They'll pin you down and rip that foetus from you using a metal hook. They will not send you to God carrying the spawn of Satan."

I grip the nail file tighter, feeling a rage I've never experienced before. "I've got a new deal," I hiss. "I kill you and hide your body under my bed." I slam my hand against his throat, feeling the skin burst open as the nail file pierces it. I drag it forward, struggling to keep a grip as blood soaks my hand. Ares's eyes widen in shock and a raspy sound leaves him as he tries to inhale while clutching his throat. I pull the file from him and blood spurts out. I panic and shove him from me, and he falls onto the floor, where he gets onto all fours and presses his hands against his throat. I wipe my bloodied hand on the bed sheet and take the file again, but this time, I stick it into the other side. When Rosey once explained this, saying I needed to be able to defend myself, she didn't warn me he'd make such awful sounds, or that there would be so much blood. And she definitely failed to mention how long it takes a person to die. I sit back on the bed, watching anxiously as Ares falls onto his side and his breathing becomes slow and shallow until, eventually, there's no sound at all.

My body is shaking uncontrollably as I lean over him to check his pulse. His chest is no longer moving, and his eyes are wide and vacant. I tap him with my foot, but he doesn't move, so I do it harder. When he still doesn't respond, I grab the sheet from the bed and kneel beside him. Covering him, I sob as the reality of what just happened hits me.

I've been staring at Ares's covered body for some time. I hear birds from outside and it breaks me from my vacant spell. I inhale sharply and begin to move, wincing as I unfold my legs from beneath me. Placing my hands on him, I push with all my might until he's under the bed. Next, I grab a second sheet and wipe up the blood staining the wood floor. I shove that under the bed too, then I stare at the dried blood on my arms and hands. I have no way of washing it off, so I sit back on my bed and cross my legs. I take the file and press my lips together before dragging the edge over my thigh, drawing blood. It's not deep enough to count for the blood on me, so I do it again, this time pushing down hard. I cry out, and pant fast like I've seen women do when they've given birth. Apparently, it helps with pain. I remove a pillowcase and wrap it around the wound, and then I wait. Someone will come soon to bring breakfast.

DICE

I stir, noting that my body aches. Memories from last night flood me as I look around the small room. Rosey took me to a meeting point, and I pretended to be drugged, but the second they placed me in their car, the fuckers injected me in the leg and I was out cold.

My hands are tied behind my back, and I'm sat on a chair in the centre of the room. My head is pounding, and my mouth is so dry, my tongue is sticking to the roof of it. "Good morning, Malachi." Joseph breezes into the room with a smile. "It's been too long."

"Fuck you," I mutter, coughing when the words scratch my throat.

"You'll be pleased to know you've arrived just in time for a very special occasion. And because you're such a valued guest, you'll get front row seats to everything."

"Again, fuck you."

"I can't pretend I'm not disappointed. Your big entrance back into my life was so dramatic and yet you failed to follow through on your plans to end me. Did you think I'd let you take my daughter right before such an important event?"

"I think you're stupid if you think my club's gonna let you get away with this."

He laughs. "Your club has its own problems. I hope you're not expecting a big rescue."

The look on his face tells me something bad has happened. "What are you talking about?"

He grins, clearly happy that I've asked. "Let's just say, things got a little hot for them in the night."

I begin to tug on my ropes. "My club has nothing to do with this, you piece of shit. If you've hurt them . . ."

"Your empty threats are boring me, Malachi. I have a wedding to prepare for."

"There are kids in that club, Joseph," I growl.

"We all have to make sacrifices, right? You took what I love, so I took what you love."

The door opens and Josephine lingers there. "Sir, we have a situation," she almost whispers, avoiding making eye contact with me.

"What's wrong, Jo? Are you too ashamed to look at me?" I snap, and she lowers her head farther. "You couldn't get enough of me when you came to the club. I seem to remember your hands on my body."

Joseph's nostrils flare. "Leave," he orders her.

"But it's Astraea," she murmurs.

I sit straighter. "What about her?" I demand.

Joseph punches me. I'm not expecting it, and my chair almost topples. "She is not your concern," he spits and then leaves, slamming the door behind him and locking it.

Fuck. Why didn't I listen to the guys? This is a suicide mission, and now, I've gotten them hurt.

CHAPTER SEVENTEEN

ASTRAEA

My father follows Josephine into my room. He takes in the blood, his eyes narrowing in on my covered thigh and then the wrist I also hacked at. He marches over, snatching the sheet from me and grabbing my arm. "That's not deep enough for the amount of blood," he says, looking around the room.

"I was trying to write you a message," I retort, "but I couldn't get enough blood to spill."

He smirks. "You can have a go later, when your blood flows freely from your throat."

I tip my head to one side, like his words don't affect me. "Really?" I ask. "Don't I get a different send off, seeing as I'm so special?" I grin at Josephine as I say it, knowing it bothers her.

"Trust me, you'll get the best. We'll make it last as long as possible. We have your boyfriend, by the way. He's excited about the wedding."

I smile. "Good. At least he'll get to see me one last time before I completely lose myself." He frowns, confused by my sentence. "I don't recognise the person you're turning me into."

"I don't have time for this riddle," he snaps. "Josephine, go and find Ares. He should have been in here ten minutes ago to take our goddess to the dressing room."

"I can take her," she offers eagerly.

He sighs heavily. "Fine. Take this in case she gets too brave." He hands her the electric rod, and she grins at me. It's time for her to get her own back.

My mother and two other women are waiting for me in a dressing room. There's a wedding dress hanging up and I eye it with distain as they lead me to a bath. I lower into the hot water, groaning as my muscles relax. The two women wash me, not caring that I wince as they scrub my skin, paying close attention to my fresh cuts. My mother watches on. "Ares is dead," I tell her.

"Sorry?" she asks.

"Ares. He's dead. I killed him."

"Don't talk ridiculous," she hisses, and the two women exchange a nervous look.

"How did I turn into this?" I ask quietly, staring at my shrivelled hands. "My life was so quiet before."

"Until you let the devil back in," Mother says, moving closer and kneeling beside the bath. She grabs my hand. "Astraea, you have to stop all this crazy talk. Your father will be so angry if he hears anymore nonsense. You always knew this day was coming. This is why you're here."

"Did you give birth to me?" I ask, looking her in the eye. "Ares said something that made me think you're not my mother."

"Does that matter? I raised you to be a perfect wife."

"But I won't get to be, will I? They'll kill me."

"But one day, you will be reunited with your husband, and you'll live for eternity in God's home. You'll live an amazing life."

I smile. "You really believe that, don't you?" She nods. "Did you always believe it?"

Something changes in her eyes and she turns to the two women. "Leave us. I can dress her." They nod and leave. "Astraea," she whispers, stroking her hand over my hair, "your father came to me when I was just a girl. He gave me so much. Why would I question him?"

"Outside of The Circle, women are allowed to think for themselves," I say. "Did you know that?"

She shrugs. "I thought so too, but my father was a terrible man. I didn't have a voice."

"Just like me," I mutter.

"I've done everything right, Astraea. God will forgive me for everything if I give you to him. I've raised you to be everything he wants. Your father is strict because he wants us to live in God's light. He rescued me from my father and his evil, wandering hands, and brought me into a world that offers forgiveness. I'm no longer that nasty, ugly little girl who deserved to be hurt." A tear slips down her cheek and she wipes it away. I've never had a moment like this with her, and she hasn't cried in front of me.

"You were a victim," I whisper, and she shrugs. "Of your father and of mine. You were vulnerable, and he took advantage. You never deserved to be hurt by the adult who was meant to love you. God would never blame you for that."

The door swings open and my father fills it. His breathing is heavy, his shoulders squared as he glares at me. I notice his blood-stained hands. "You killed him," he growls.

"He was trying to have sex with me," I spit.

"So, you killed him?" he roars, like that isn't a good enough excuse. "You let that devil have you but not Ares?"

"You weren't lying," Mother whispers, and I shake my head. "You killed Ares."

"He was going to do what your father did to you. It's wrong."

My father rushes forward, almost knocking her out of the way. She scoots back and flinches when he grips me by the hair and hauls me effortlessly from the bath. "Get the dress," he orders her. She does, and I feel the small connection we just had slip away. "You are going through with the ceremony today and there will be no more fuss," he tells me. He wraps his arms around me, lifting me up so my mother can bring the dress up my body. He forces each arm into the correct sleeve and spins me to face him while Mother fastens the pearl buttons. "I'm going to enjoy watching the life drain from you," he whispers, running his finger along my jaw.

"I'll be sure to put on a great show," I promise him with a smile.

It's not like a normal wedding. Not like the one Rylee showed me of her and Maverick on her phone. I stand in the doorway to another room in the house. It's been done out like a church with seats on either side of an aisle and a cross at the front with a makeshift altar. Lining the aisle are the Lords in full cloaks with their hoods up. I shudder at the memory of them last night. There are no guests or family filling the seats, no happy, smiling faces to watch me take my vows.

At the altar stands the man I'm supposed to marry. The stranger. He leers at me as he watches me approach, and when his eyes flick to the left, I follow them and gasp. *Dice.* Our eyes connect and I lose all control, pulling from my father to reach him. Instead, I'm yanked back hard, almost knocking the breath from me. "Focus," Father hisses close to my ear. The Lords seat themselves in the seats and a vicar gives me a nervous smile. He must be here against his will too.

Dice smiles. "It's gonna be okay, Six."

"You don't understand," I cry, trying again to break free so I can get to him.

"Astraea!" Father snaps, squeezing my wrist so hard, it makes a popping noise and I scream out in pain. "I warned you already."

I ignore him. I have to say the words just in case they're my last. He should know what we created together. "I'm pregnant, Dice," I whisper.

He inhales sharply, and something changes in his expression. "Pregnant?" he repeats. I nod, offering a small smile.

"Is this a joke?" snaps Robert angrily.

"She's just trying to delay the ceremony," Father says calmly. "I've done all the tests."

"Is she even pure?" he snaps.

"No," I yell.

Father squeezes my wrist tighter, and I whimper. "She is pure, as promised. Now, shall we proceed?"

"You're a liar!" I scream. I stare at Robert desperately. "I am pregnant. I have had sex."

A sharp slap knocks me off my feet. "If you know what's good for you, you'll shut that evil mouth of yours and do what you're here for," Father warns.

Robert steps closer, offering his hand to pull me up. I ignore it, pushing to my feet unaided. "Are we proceeding?" asks the vicar.

"I really wanted to wait for the best part," comes a voice I know so well. I almost cry with relief when Rosey appears at the doorway and Dice grins. I don't think I've ever seen him happy to hear Rosey's voice. "Yah know the part, right?" she asks, beginning to skip towards us. "Where you ask if anyone objects, and I run in dramatically and scream 'I do'. But you ruined it with the slap." She pauses halfway down the aisle and looks at the Lords sitting in their seats with their heads bowed. "No one told me this was fancy dress," she adds. "You look like idiots."

DICE

Relief floods me. "I was hoping you'd still be naked," says Rosey, smirking in my direction. "They've ruined all my plans today, and you know how upset I get when things don't go my way."

"You took your time," I hiss, tugging at my restraints so she can come and cut them.

Joseph grabs Astraea and holds her against him. "What the hell is going on?"

"I would have been here sooner, but we had shit to deal with. It's not all about you, Dice," says Rosey, ignoring Joseph and moving towards me. She then turns to him and narrows her eyes. "And for the record, Captain Crazy, you hit the wrong building. We own that empty warehouse, but we don't live there. What do you think we are, animals?" She rolls her eyes and turns back to me. "They firebombed the wrong place."

There's unrest amongst the Lords, and Joseph turns his attention to them. "Have you all lost your ability to help?" he yells. "Someone lock the doors. No one is stopping this ceremony." He grips Astraea by the throat. "God will strike us all down if this doesn't go ahead. Lords, kill these outsiders before they ruin everything," he commands.

Rosey slowly spins to face the Lords. "Well, you heard the man, help," she snaps impatiently. They stand, removing their hoods. "Oh crap," she adds, turning back to Joseph, "I forgot to mention, The Perished Riders are in town." I stare in disbelief at Maverick, Ghost, Scar, Copper, and the rest of the motherfucking bikers I love so much as they shrug out of the ridiculous robes.

"Fuck, I've never been so pleased to see your ugly faces," I say, sighing with relief.

"We wanted to make you sweat," says Grim. "It was a suicide mission, right?"

I grin. "Nah, I had it all under control."

"What the hell is happening?" yells Robert, his eyes scanning the room in confusion.

"You're not getting laid after all," singsongs Rosey. "You sick motherfucker."

Joseph backs away, holding Astraea to him. "I'll kill her if you don't let us out of here," he warns. Astraea gasps, trying to claw his fingers from her throat. Rosey cuts the rope holding my wrists, and I rush towards them. "I mean it," he yells, looking around frantically for a weapon. He shoves Astraea hard, and she falls against me, rubbing her throat. "Pregnant," I whisper, kissing her on the head. "I'm gonna be a fucking dad." Tears fill her eyes. "I love you," I tell her, right before gently pushing her towards Scar. "Just give me a minute to put an end to this." I need to finish this once and for all, so we can move forward.

I advance on Joseph. Each step forward I take, he takes another back. "You know you're gonna die now. You should make your peace with God," I tell him. Making a quick grab, I catch his upper arm and haul him closer. I grin in his face before holding up the set of dice. "I don't even have to roll them to know what I'm gonna do to you," I hiss. He opens his mouth to speak, and I ram the dice into it, slamming it closed and holding it until he has no choice but to swallow. He begins to choke, and I drag him over to the fake altar. The vicar steps to one side, a horrified expression on his face.

"Do you know how long I've waited?" I ask, holding Joseph on his back with my hand over his mouth and nose. I watch his face turn pale and his lips blue. "But I need to know, do you really believe in God?" He kicks out, desperately trying to get his mouth free. "Because I don't think you do. I think you killed those women and children in cold blood. In a sick, perverted fantasy. I think it's what you did to my mother, and it's what you were gonna do to your own daughter." I place my knee on his chest, and Rosey passes me her knife. "I hope you rot in hell." I hold the blade against his throat. "I'll see you there and we can spend eternity discussing this moment, but until then, know that I won." I slit his throat, deep enough to sever his spinal cord. I release his head, and he hits the red carpet with a thud. "Get out of here," I tell the vicar. "If you tell anyone about this, I'll come for you." He nods, rushing out frantically.

I glance over to where Robert Shaw is slumped and Ghost is wiping his knife clean. "I wanted to get at least one kill," Rosey is complaining to Mav. "And Dice used my knife, which was just rude."

"I let you come, ain't that enough?" asks Mav.

I can't help but smile. She loves drama but hates not being involved in the club more. I make a mental note to raise the issue with the guys in church because she works just as hard as the brothers.

Scar comes over and leans in close. "I-I couldn't s-s-stop her," he whispers. I frown, looking around to see no sign of Six. "C-come," he adds, leading me from the room and up the winding staircase. "She saw the b-bodies first," he continues to fill me in as I follow. "Outside." I glance out the window at the top of the stairs to see the Lords' bodies spread out over the gravel, no longer wearing robes, their crimson blood flowing freely around them. A satisfaction passes over me, and Scar tugs my arm to remind me we're looking for Astraea.

I hear a frustrated cry and run towards it. I stop in the doorway to a bedroom and take in Astraea's blood-stained white dress. She looks from her hands to me and then to the body of Josephine and then her mother. "Six?"

Her lips quiver, and she inhales before whispering, "She killed my mother."

I nod, stepping closer and carefully removing the blade she's gripping tightly in her hand. "Okay," I murmur, passing the knife to Scar. "Are you okay?" I dip my head slightly to catch her eye. "Did she hurt you?" She shakes her head.

"How did we get here?" she whispers, her face full of confusion.

I frown, wondering if she's temporarily lost her mind after the stress she's been through. "They took you," I explain.

"I don't mean that. How did I turn into this? Are they right? Is the devil inside of me?" She begins to shake, staring hard at her stained hands.

"No, Six. We talked about this. It was them or you."

Maverick comes in. "We gotta go, brother. This place needs to burn."

Astraea seems to break out of her trance. "What about all the girls?"

"Some have run away, and we don't have the time to look for them. But some are with Rosey on their way to a meeting point. She gave an anonymous tip to a support worker who will get them the help they need, but right now, we have to cut all ties with this, or the police will come for us."

I see the panic in her eyes and rush to reassure her. "We're gonna be okay, Six, and so are they. They'll get the help they need. But all the men, all those who hurt them, are gone. They'll never be able to hurt anyone else."

CHAPTER EIGHTEEN

ASTRAEA

The blood doesn't wash off easily. I scrub my skin until I see my own blood, and it's only when Dice steps into the shower fully clothed and removes the nail brush from my hands that I realise I'm sobbing. "It doesn't come off," I tell him. "It's stained my skin."

He takes my hands and holds them up for inspection. "Baby, they're clean. See?" But they don't feel clean. "I want you to speak to your therapist today."

I shake my head in protest. "No. I don't want to talk about any of this. I don't want anyone to know what I did."

"She won't tell anyone. She knows the club, and she knows how things go down."

"That doesn't make me feel better," I snap, tugging my hands free. "How do you do it? How do you switch your emotions off?"

He smiles sadly. "Easy. When people like your father leave this world, I breathe a little easier. What we did was rid the world of evil. He'll never rape another woman. He'll never get the chance to trick them into that life, and he won't be able to use women as his personal breeding machines."

I stare down at my feet. "My mother was opening up to me," I tell him. "She told me things that made me understand why she wanted to believe my father so desperately. She was a victim too."

"Did you go back up there to save her?" he asks, and I nod. When I ran back to that room, I didn't know how I was going to convince her to leave with us, but I wanted to try. Seeing Josephine standing over her like that, it broke my heart, because she didn't deserve that. She was taken in by my father just like we all were.

Dice places his hand over my stomach. "I can't believe it," he whispers with a smile. "We made a baby."

"He might have been lying," I point out. "Ares told me he did a test."

"Ares, your brother?" I nod. "What happened to him? Was he with the Lords?" He suddenly looks worried, thinking he let one get away.

"I . . . I, erm . . ." I take a shaky breath before looking him in the eyes. "He was going to hurt me, so I stopped him."

Dice looks concerned. "How did you stop him?"

"I stole a metal nail file. I killed him. I stabbed him in the throat like Rosey told me."

"Rosey?" he repeats, sounding more confused.

"I think she saw this day coming. She told me I could use everyday things as a weapon, even a key. The nail file was all I could find."

He gently rubs my arms, smiling kindly. "At least she's good for something," he jokes. "You did good today, Six. Better than I thought you ever would. You can survive out there, yah know, you proved that. And we'll get the pregnancy confirmed. If there's no baby, we'll just have to try harder." He gives me a wink.

Dice turns off the shower and grabs a towel. He wraps me up and sits me on the closed toilet seat while he strips out of his wet clothes and wraps himself in one. "We need to talk about things, Six." He looks me in the eye, and his expression is suddenly serious. "You ran away, putting yourself—and my kid—in danger. I wanna know what the fuck you were thinking." He takes my hand and pulls me to stand, tucking a piece of stray hair behind my ear. He's pissed at me but not in a way that makes my blood run cold. I don't fear him. He places a gentle kiss on my nose. "But first, I gotta take care of you."

He leads me back into the bedroom and sits me in the chair by the window. He then proceeds to plug in a hair dryer and sets about drying my wet hair.

I relax, closing my eyes and enjoying the feel of his fingers running through my hair. It feels good being back here with him again.

I wake with a start. The room is in darkness. A panic rises in my chest as I reach for the lamp, and then I realise I'm at the club and I'm safe, and my heart rate slows a little. But Dice is gone, and the side of the bed where he lay earlier is cold. I grab his discarded shirt, pulling it on and making my way downstairs. The club is silent, but as I move towards the main room, low voices catch my attention. They're coming from inside the room the men usually meet in. Church, I think Dice calls it. I push the door in time to hear Dice say, "I'm making her mine before any more crazy shit happens."

"Isn't it over?" I ask, and they all turn to me in surprise. "Or is there more crazy coming our way?"

Dice rises to his feet. "Six, you ain't allowed in here."

Mav pats Dice on the arm and shakes his head. Dice sits back down, and Mav smiles at me. "I bet you've had enough of rules. Come in, Six. Sit with us."

Grim pulls out the chair between him and Scar. "How are yah feeling, darlin'?" asks Copper.

I lower into the seat, and Scar pushes me closer to the large table. Dice narrows his eyes, not happy I'm between his brothers rather than sat beside him. "Tired," I admit. "Exhausted, actually."

"Yeah, it gets you like that," Mav agrees.

"Why'd yah leave us, Six?" asks Grim.

"I overheard Dice," I mutter, lowering my head but watching Dice's reaction through my lashes. "He was telling Mav I needed to be moved from the club. I thought he didn't want me here anymore."

"Shit, Six, that's why you ran?" snaps Dice. "Why didn't you just come and talk to me? I would have explained what I meant, cos I sure as shit wasn't tryin' to get rid of you."

"I didn't want to be a burden."

He stands and rounds the table, turning my chair to face him and crouching down. "I wanted you to taste freedom, Six. I was worried you'd jumped from one crazy bastard to another. Cos, shit, I want you more than I've ever wanted anything and that scares the shit outta me. I don't wanna keep you here when there's so much of the world you ain't seen."

"After everything I've been through, this is freedom," I reassure him. "Being with you is freedom."

"Well, I'm glad you feel like that, cos you're staying with me from this second on. Don't ever leave me like that, Six. I can't go through it again."

I nod, smiling as a happy tear rolls down my cheek. "So, you want me around?"

He grins, pressing his forehead against mine. "I love you, Six. I always have, and I'll never not want you around."

"I love you too," I admit. The men begin to make their exit, leaving us alone. "I'm sorry I left. Is that how The Circle got to you? Were you looking for me?"

"No, I went there voluntarily," he admits, and I gasp. "They put a price on my head, and Rosey took the job. We pretended that she hunted me down, drugged me, and took me to them. It was the only option we had to get you back. We didn't know where you were. The only clue we had was Cam's body. If that hadn't been found, we probably wouldn't have realised they'd taken you."

"Josephine shot him," I mutter, remembering the look on Cam's face as he took his last breath. I bury my face in my hands and begin to cry again. "He called her to help us, and she took us right back to The Circle. The look on his face when we realised what she'd done . . ." Another sob escapes me. "All these people who died because of me."

He grips my wrists and tugs them from my face. "Not because of you, Six. Because of them. It was all because of them."

"Cam didn't want to leave the club, but I made him," I confess. "He was trying to help me, and he died because of it."

"He died because Josephine shot him. One way or another, The Circle was determined to get you back. They didn't care who was in their way, and if you carry the burden of their sins, you'll slowly kill yourself. Cam loved you, and all he ever wanted, was for you to be happy. We can't change the past, Six. We have to move forward."

One month later...

DICE

I smile at the delight on Astraea's face as she watches people rushing along Oxford Street. It's been a month since she came home to the club, and it's like she's always been here. But it's special moments like this that I love the most. I get to watch all her firsts. Her first time on a train, her first taste of chicken curry in an Indian restaurant, the way her eyes sparkled when she saw Chinatown. And then there's the tourist things Rylee insisted I do with her, her favourite being the museums. She can't get enough of reading and learning, and seeing her so absorbed in life is the best feeling ever.

Darkness is setting in, and I have a table booked on the London Eye in just an hour. We walk through London's streets because Astraea loves being surrounded by people, even strangers in the street. There are times in the night when she wakes screaming, paralysed by her nightmares and guilt, and we walk. We take to the streets because London is never asleep and it relaxes her to be amongst the hustle and bustle.

When we get to the large white wheel, she strains her neck and stares up at it. "You booked this?" She'd pointed it out several times in passing before now, but I was saving it for this moment. I nod, and she squeals excitedly.

We're shown into our own cart, where a butler awaits to serve us non-alcoholic champagne. We take a glass each and then sit at the table set for two. "Happy?" I ask her, and she nods, too busy looking around to take in my questions. "Excited for tomorrow?" I add, and she nods again. It's our first scan of the baby. After getting the pregnancy confirmed a couple of weeks ago, the doc recommended we have the scan to determine the due date.

I let her take in her surroundings, following her when she stands to see out over London. It's beautiful at night with all the lights twinkling, and I knew she'd love it.

"I love you so much," she gushes, taking my hand. "Isn't it gorgeous out there? This has to be the best view over London."

"At the risk of sounding corny, I haven't noticed, I'm too busy watching you."

She laughs. "Rosey would rip into you for that."

"Seeing how you look at life, Six, it lights me up. You love everything with such enthusiasm."

"It's freedom," she says. "I've never been so happy and relaxed and calm. I'll never be able to thank you enough for setting me free."

"I waited all these years," I continue. "I knew I loved you from when we were just kids. It was always you, Astraea." She turns to look at me, noting the tone of the conversation and how serious I sound. "Which is why I wanted to ask you," I lower to one knee and hold out the ring as she gasps, completely shocked, "if you'd marry me?"

"Yes," she whispers. "Yes, of course, I will."

She drops to my level, wrapping her arms around me. "I love you," I tell her again, relief flooding me.

She pulls back to look at the ring. "It's so pretty." I take it from the box and smile as it glides into place. "Oh my god, I can't believe we're getting married."

"I'll make you happy every single day," I promise her. "You'll always be my priority, and no one will ever hurt you again."

She places a gentle kiss against my lips. "I love you."

ASTRAEA

The happy little bubble I find myself in pushes all the bad away and I focus on the wedding and baby plans. We haven't set a date yet because we want to see when our bundle of joy is going to arrive, so as I lie on the bed, staring up at the ceiling, I pray to God everything is well. The trauma of being beaten all those weeks ago has been playing on my mind, but I didn't tell my fears to Dice, because he would have paid for a private scan to put my mind at rest. He does everything he can to make me happy.

The sonographer squeezes some cold gel onto my stomach, bringing my attention back to the room. Dice holds my hand tightly, and his whole demeanour is tense. Maybe he has the same worries as me. The scanner is pressed onto my stomach, and I turn my head to look at the black screen. It suddenly comes alive with a grainy picture that looks nothing like I expected it to. She moves it around, pushing in places, and then she points to a small black spot on the screen. "This is the heartbeat," she says, smiling.

I peer closer, frowning. "I can't see it. Why can't I see it?"

She flicks a button on the monitor and a sound fills the room. "Then listen," she tells me.

"That's the baby?" asks Dice as the fast beat fills the room, and she nods. "Fuck, that's our baby," he repeats, grinning at me.

"So, everything is fine?" I ask, finding it hard to believe.

"Everything looks great. I'll take some measurements and work out how far along you are." She falls silent, clicking buttons and moving the scanner.

I turn to Dice. "I was so worried," I whisper.

He brushes the hair from my face and gently kisses me on the forehead. "Me too, Six. But you heard her, everything is fine."

"Okay, so, it looks like you're around nine weeks," interrupts the sonographer. "We'll book you in again for another scan in a few weeks and get you assigned to a midwife."

The girls are waiting for us to return, and the second I step into the clubhouse, I'm dragged away by Rylee to join them all. "Nine weeks," I announce, waving the pictures around. Hadley snatches them for a closer look.

"So, can we arrange this wedding now?" asks Meli.

Dice comes up behind me, wrapping his arms around my waist. "She wants to wait until after the baby," he tells them, and Meli glares at me.

"I don't wanna be a fat bride," I complain.

"Curves are beautiful, especially ones that your child gave you," she retorts.

Dice runs his hands over my flat stomach. "You're not showing yet, maybe we could do it now?"

Meli claps her hands in delight. "Yes, that's a great idea."

"Now?" I repeat. "But I don't have anything organised."

Dice turns me in his arms and tips my chin back to look at him. "All we need is a bride and groom, Six. I just want you to be my wife. I don't need the fancy shit for that."

I smile, kissing him. "You always say the right things."

"I'll call the vicar and see when he can get you in," says Rylee, rushing off to the office.

"But if you want the fancy shit, that's fine too. I can wait," Dice continues.

I shake my head. "I just want you."

Rylee reappears a few minutes later. "How about tomorrow?" she asks, covering the mouthpiece on her mobile.

My eyes widen. "Tomorrow?"

"He's free. Mav said he can sort a licence in time. You just have to say yes."

I glance at Dice, who nods, grinning wide. I shrug. "Yes."

The women clap with delight and then everyone begins panicking and barking orders at each other, realising we have less than twenty-four hours to plan a wedding. Dice picks me up and heads off towards the stairs. "Where the hell are you going with our bride?" shouts Meli, rushing after us.

"*My bride*, Meli. Sort out whatever you want, but I need to be alone with Six."

"You're giving me full control?" she asks.

"Complete control," he throws over his shoulder.

"But you shouldn't really see the bride before the big day," she says.

"Meli, I promised her I'd never leave her again and I'm keeping that promise."

"But it's bad luck," she argues.

"I think we've had all the bad luck we're gonna have. Now, go and organise the wedding, you're running out of time."

She shrugs, sighing heavily but walking away. "You're so bossy," I whisper, snuggling into him. He kisses me on the head and carries me up to our room.

CHAPTER NINETEEN

ASTRAEA

"Are you nervous?" asks Meli as she puts the finishing touches to my makeup. I shake my head. I spent the entire night wrapped in Dice's arms, and I've never felt more relaxed and calm in my life. For the first time, I'm certain I'm on the right path, the one I was always supposed to be on.

"She's marrying the love of her life, what's to be nervous about?" asks Rosey.

Meli rolls her eyes. "You don't understand human emotion, so you wouldn't get it."

"I'm not a robot," she argues. "I just don't know why anyone would be nervous on their wedding day when you're about to marry the one person you want to spend forever with."

"Forever is a long time," agrees Meli thoughtfully.

"Fuck," mutters Hadley, "are you trying to scare her?"

"Hadley," Meli gasps, "you never curse."

"She's been spending too long around Grim," cuts in Rylee. "We never see you anymore," she adds.

Hadley grins. "He wants another baby. It's keeping us busy."

"That's great news," says Nelly. "We're growing the club just like Mav envisioned."

"Speaking of which," says Rylee, smirking.

We all turn to stare at her, and she places her hand over her stomach. "I'm not allowed to tell anyone, so I won't say the actual words, but you get the idea."

"You're pregnant?" gasps Meli, and Rylee nods, biting her lower lip to stop her huge smile spreading.

"Oh my god," cries Hadley, and we all end up in one big hug.

"Mav is really cautious. It's very early days, and he wants to keep it a secret a little longer, but I'm so excited," says Rylee.

"You're going to be pregnant together," Nelly points out.

Rylee hooks an arm around my shoulders. "We can stick together against our overprotective men because I feel like Mav is gonna be overbearing."

"I can't believe my brother is going to be a dad," says Meli.

"He's great with Ella," Rylee points out. "I can't wait to see how he is with a newborn though."

"Ella isn't Mav's?" I ask. He's always so good with her, I didn't realise.

Rylee shakes her head. "No, remember, I told you I escaped an abusive relationship, it was from Ella's dad. She was only three at the time, so she doesn't really remember much, and she calls Mav 'Dad'."

"That's sweet," I reply, thinking how lucky she is to have found a great man to raise her daughter with. I wish my mum had done the same.

"Anyway, let's get you in the dress," she says, unzipping the bag containing the dress she wore for her own wedding. It was too short notice to get my own, and I appreciate the girls rallying around to make sure I have the perfect day.

DICE

"Are you nervous?" asks Mav from beside me.

I shake my head. "I've been waiting for this day since I was a kid. I've never been so sure of anyone in my life."

Michael, the vicar and one of my brothers, stands before me, waiting patiently for Astraea's arrival. When the doors open and our guests stand, I breathe a sigh of relief. I didn't doubt she'd turn up, but a part of me expected her to have a last-minute panic, she questions everything since coming home. The therapist said it's normal. She's had a lot of trauma, and she's working through it. Being lied to her entire life makes her not able to trust herself or her decisions.

I turn and watch as she makes her way towards me. She holds onto Copper's arm, keeping her eyes fixed on me, and the second she's close enough, I pull her to me, kissing her. "We're not at that part yet," says Michael with a laugh.

"Then get on with it," I retort.

And he does. The ceremony is short, like we both wanted it to be. We've had enough of this sort of thing recently, and if it was up to me, we'd have skipped this whole part altogether, but it was important to Astraea that we did things properly. And with our baby on the way, I understood that.

Certain traditions, I insisted we keep, like our first dance. Mainly because I wanted everyone to see that Six was officially mine. I wanted my brothers to watch me dance with the most beautiful woman in the world and know she belonged to me. The other was our tattoos. It took some convincing to get Astraea to agree, but it was the one thing I wasn't going to budge on. It's club tradition and the only thing I'll ever insist she does.

I gently kiss my name scribed in black ink on her wrist, and she stirs. When her eyes flutter open, she smirks. "Not again. I need food."

I laugh. I could spend twenty-four-seven buried inside her, but she's right, it's been a few hours since we snuck away from the wedding reception, and my pregnant wife needs to eat every hour or she turns into the Hulk. *Wife*. I love the way it sounds. "I had the best day today," I tell her.

She wraps the sheet around her to stop my wandering hands, and I smirk. "Me too. When I was getting dressed this morning, surrounded by the girls, I felt like I was home. It's like I'm a part of something, finally. And not like it was at The Circle. This is like a real family, where everyone looks out for each other."

"The club's been like that for most of us. We've all needed to be a part of something and that's what makes us the perfect family. We don't take it for granted because we know what it feels like to have nothing."

"I love it here. I can't wait to raise our daughter surrounded by all this love."

He grins, pulling the sheet from me and resting his head on my stomach. "You know it's a boy in there, Six, don't make me insane."

"But if it's a girl, we get to keep trying for a boy," I remind him.

He climbs over me, resting between my legs. "There'll be plenty of practising, Six, don't you worry about that."

But I know she isn't worried. She never has to worry about anything again because I'll spend my life protecting her and our children. They say everything happens for a reason. Mum dying gave me an escape, and without that, I would have grown up to be the same as all the other men in The Circle.

Meeting Astraea was my destiny and saving her was my mission. Loving her is my choice, one I'll continue to choose forever.

THE END

Read on for a look at the next book – Arthur

Arthur - A mafia spin off from The Perished Riders MC

PROLOGUE
ROSEY

I grab the tie belonging to my target. He's attached to it still. He thinks it's a game and willingly follows me through the crowds of people. I did my research and know where all the blind spots are in this place, so I keep my head lowered as we pass under a security camera. I'm pretty sure my dazzling sequined dress will blind any images anyway.

"Fuck, you're so hot," he growls, grabbing my hips and thrusting himself against my behind. I roll my eyes. Does this behaviour actually turn people on? His wandering hands reach around my hips and the heat of his body presses against my back as I continue to lead him to our final destination.

He doesn't question how I know my way around this nightclub as I lead him up some back stairs. Of course he doesn't, because his end game is different than mine. All he's thinking about is getting his dick sucked. All I'm thinking about is getting the job done so I can go home and get my pyjamas on. Maybe I'll catch Ollie awake. Since he turned ten, he's been trying to push the boundaries and stay up later. I give my head a shake. I can't afford to mess this up because there's big money waiting to be wired into my account.

I push the fire exit door, and we step out onto the roof. This guy's a typical drunk rich boy, hands in my bra, grabbing my tits way too hard to do anything but repulse me. I have yet to find a guy who knows exactly how to touch me to get me going. I manage to get him towards the ledge and I peer over. The streets below are busy and I don't wanna risk him hurting anyone, so I move to the other ledge, making it into a game of chase. I even throw a giggle his way. He falls for of it, desperate for the fuck. Wanker.

I stop, peering over the wall. It's quieter down there, but not so quiet he won't be spotted. His body slams against mine, and the air leaves my lungs. "Fuck, I want you so bad," he growls into my hair, his hands grabbing at my chest again. He's strong for his size, and for a second, I'm transported back to another time. One when I was helpless against the wandering hands and the stale breath near my neck. He yanks my skirt up hard and spins me away from him, bending me over the ledge. This is not how it's meant to go.

"Aren't you married?" I ask as he kicks my legs apart.

"I sleep on the couch," he mutters, taking a fistful of my hair and dragging his wet mouth down my neck.

I'm grossed out. If this was a real hook-up, I'd be so turned off, I'd have to stop it. "Jolene, right?"

I feel him stiffen, and not in the turned-on way. "Huh?"

"Your wife. It's Jolene, right?" He takes an unsteady step back, and I turn to face him, smiling as I lower my dress. "A few pointers . . . not that you'll ever need them again." I take his tie for a second time, and we walk in a circle until his back is to the ledge. "Your hands, way too rough. No woman wants to feel like a slab of meat. And the thrusting . . . oh god, the thrusting . . . I mean, all men do it, right? But why? What makes you think any woman, especially a stranger, wants you to thrust your fucking cock into her back? It's not sexy," I say, throwing my arms in the air, then I place my fingers against my temple.

"Is it like a primal thing? Yah know, *hey, look how big my cock is*? Cos I have to tell you, it's not actually what we think. Just then when you prodded me, my first thought was, gross, obviously. But then I thought about getting home to my own bed and snuggling down to watch Netflix. Is that what you were hoping for when you shoved your erection against me?" He shakes his head slowly, his eyes darting around in panic. "If you really are sleeping on the couch, no wonder. Jolene must be sick of your caveman attitude to sex."

"What's going on?" he asks. "Are you crazy?"

I nod. "A little. It's childhood trauma, apparently. My therapist says I can be fixed, but honestly, I quite like me. Why fix what works? Anyway, back to Jolene. Do you want to know what a woman really wants?" He shrugs, looking around helplessly again. "She wants love, Jeremy. She wants attention. She does not want a cheating husband who thrusts his dick into people's backs, hoping for a quick fuck where I probably wouldn't have even come because, let's face it, Jezza, you're going to be shit in bed, aren't you?"

"I'm sorry, okay. I've never done this before. I don't usually pick up women."

I laugh and it echoes around the rooftop. "I almost feel bad for you. Maybe you weren't loved enough as a kid. Or maybe you settled down too young. You've clearly never been shown how to treat a woman. Now, I could humour your lies, but it's not in my nature. Before you hit the bottom, I want you to think of these people." I open my bag and reveal his iPad. He frowns, not comprehending it's his because he knows he locked it away in the boot of his car. Along with all the dark clothing and the balaclava he uses. It was so cliché.

I begin to scroll through the photos of his victims, photos only he's seen, and the penny begins to drop. He recognises his iPad and his face pales. "You really are a sick fuck. She looks about sixteen. I mean, you've ruined her life forever. Do you think about that when you walk away? Do you consider the damage you've done to a sixteen-year-old virgin? She'll hate men forever. Trust me, I know."

"She . . . she was on . . . I mean, she wanted to meet me."

"Yes, she was on a dating app. But fuck's sake, Jezza, she's sixteen, and you're what, forty? You should know better. You're the adult. And she never joined that app to meet old men who would ruin her life. In her naivety, she thought she'd find a good guy."

"She wanted it rough," he spits.

"No, she didn't. There you go again, reading the room wrong. Does she look happy in this picture, Jeremy?" I thrust the iPad closer, and he turns his head away. The girl in the picture is tied up and sobbing. Her eyes are swollen from tears, and she's covered in bite marks and bruises. "Is that what you were going to do to me tonight?" He shakes his head. "Of course not, because I'm not a kid. I can fight back. You know, Jolene knows what you've done."

His eyes widen in shock. "How?"

"She's very important, or should I say, her family is. Why would you risk it?"

"Did they hire you? Are you here to scare me off, because I'm not leaving my marriage without a pay-out."

I groan. "She said you'd say that."

"You spoke to my wife?"

I put the iPad back in my bag. "The thing is, Jezza," I move closer, "she doesn't want to divorce you."

He looks relieved. "Okay, she wants to work it out. I can stop. I'll stop."

I give him a pitying smile. "Nope. I think she's tired of the shit sex and covering your arse with her brothers." I grimace. "They really don't like you, do they?"

He visibly swallows. "I don't understand."

"Enjoy it," I tell him, getting a good grip on his shoulders. He frowns, and I shove him hard. "In hell," I add as he falls backwards over the wall onto the street below.

I grab my bag and pull out a jumper and tracksuit bottoms. I slip them on and tuck my hair into a cap. I can hear screaming below as I gather everything up and make a run for the fire exit. I slam it closed and rush down the stairs, all the way to the ground level. I push through some swing doors into a kitchen area. It's not been used for years, since the restaurant was bought out by the nightclub owners. I push out the exit and into a back alley which leads to the street beside the club. There are couples kissing and I dodge past them, breaking out into the busy street.

There's chaos as I calmly pass the nightclub entrance. The customers who are normally queuing outside to get in are all around the other side of the building, and as I pass, I see them crowded around Jeremy's lifeless body. Mobile phones are alight in the air as they hold them high above each other's heads to catch a glimpse. The youth of today have no compassion.

"What's happened?" I ask a girl who's sobbing into her hands.

"A man just jumped from the roof."

"Fuck. Is he okay?"

She wails, shaking her head. "No, he's dead."

A note from me to you

I don't know where Dice's story came from. I've never thought about writing a story involving cults, although they do fascinate me. When I researched the topic, my mind was blown. There are so many out there, past and present. I began his story and changed it so many times until Astraea came to me, and their story flowed from that moment on.

If you enjoyed their story, I'd love it if you'd leave a review. It helps little authors like me out, so much.

You can also follow me on social media. I'm literally everywhere, but here's my linktr.ee to make it easier. https://linktr.ee/NicolaJaneUK

I'm a UK author, based in Nottinghamshire. I live with my husband of many years, our two teenage boys and our four little dogs. I write MC and Mafia romance with plenty of drama and chaos. I also love to read similar books. Before I became a full-time author, I was a teaching assistant working in a primary school.

If you'd like to follow my writing journey, join my readers group on Facebook, the link is above. You can also use that link if you're a book blogger, I'd love you to sign up to my team.

Books from this Author

Riggs' Ruin https://mybook.to/RiggsRuin
Capturing Cree https://mybook.to/CapturingCree
Wrapped in Chains https://mybook.to/WrappedinChains
Saving Blu https://mybook.to/SavingBlu
Riggs' Saviour https://mybook.to/RiggsSaviour
Taming Blade https://mybook.to/TamingBlade
Misleading Lake https://mybook.to/MisleadingLake
Surviving Storm https://mybook.to/SurvivingStorm
Ravens Place https://mybook.to/RavensPlace
Playing Vinn https://mybook.to/PlayingVinn

Other books by Nicola Jane:
The Perished Riders MC
Maverick https://mybook.to/Maverick-Perished
Scar https://mybook.to/Scar-Perished

Grim https://mybook.to/Grim-Perished
Ghost https://mybook.to/GhostBk4
Dice https://mybook.to/DiceBk5

The Hammers MC (Splintered Hearts Series)
Cooper https://mybook.to/CooperSHS
Kain https://mybook.to/Kain
Tanner https://mybook.to/TannerSH

Printed in Dunstable, United Kingdom